Roadrunners Rock!

A celebration of students
and their achievements in writing

**Rock Spring Elementary School
McDonough,GA**

2009-2010

Published by

Pen & Publish

Bloomington, Indiana
(812) 837-9226
info@PenandPublish.com
www.PenandPublish.com

ISBN: 978-0-9844600-2-1

This book is printed on acid free paper.

Printed in the USA

Acknowledgement
Ms. Tracy DiSario
Principal, Rock Spring Elementary School

A special thank you goes to Mrs. Susan Murdock, third grade teacher, who envisioned this publication and whose infallible attention to detail and dedication made this collection a reality. At Rock Spring Elementary, we value the art of writing. This publication is a tribute to all the hard work our students and teachers have given to the writing process during the 2009-2010 school year.

This book is dedicated to our present and future authors.

Dedication
Dr. Toni Obenauf
Assistant Principal, Rock Spring Elementary School

This book is dedicated to the teachers of
Rock Spring Elementary.

The Rock Spring teachers have encouraged our students to share their stories and creations with us. They have worked hard to teach ways of communicating stories and special information using a variety of methods. One method was the compilation of this book, which would not be possible without the dedication of our fabulous teachers.

A teacher's purpose is not to create students in his or her own image, but to develop students who can create their own image. Thank you for spending the time and effort necessary to strengthen our students' minds.

"We do not believe in ourselves until someone reveals that deep inside us something is valuable, worth listening to, worthy of our trust, sacred to our touch. Once we believe in ourselves we can risk curiosity, wonder, spontaneous delight or any experience that reveals the human spirit. ..." ~ E. E. Cummings

Table of Contents

Chapter 1
Kindergarten Rocks

Kindergarten (Unedited)
Ms. Hamrick

It is snowiin at are has. – *Asa S.*

Green Wilma is a fg. – *Jedea C.*

Godelox has the chicken pox. – *Georgia R.*

Family is impoortant. My family is fun. – *Jake H.*

I'm goig to get a rose. – *Esther R.*

help. (In response to the earthquake in Haiti.) – *Dillon L.*

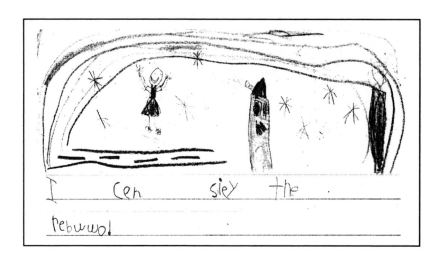

I rock. – *Izsak S.*

Me and my sisr are pan in the soleg. – *Rhiannon B.*

Logan is a playin Logan. – *Logan G.*

I want to go at Grandmas house. – *Mark R.*

I am pany basktbol. – *Ethan C.*

Moiy dogs nem is Teird. I am Nia. – *Nia G.*

Kindergarten (Unedited)
Ms. Cash

You can bild a snowman. – *Kaitlin D.*

In witr you can bld a snoman. – *Lana H.*

In winter I play video games. – *McKinley W.*

I can see sno at nit. I can play atsid. – *Taylor A.*

I can see ic ascd. I can play ase. – *Brianna R.*

I can play in the snow. – *Travis B.*

I like to go to play in the sow and I like to play in the sow and play in the huhs. – *Kendall B.*

I like to play in the snuo. – *Ayden H.*

Sometimes it might rain when it snows. – *Caiden M.*

You can play in sno if you play. – *Hunter S.*

It snos in d winter. I pla in d sno. Sno man ome! – *Chandler B.*

My dogs fod bol had tow pesis ov ice. – *Lauren S.*

It snowd my houes. I look at my wido. I wus so happy wi it snow. – *Alexandria S.*

I am mcic a snoman. – *Cameron T.*

Me and my dad mad a soneman! – *Elliott L*

Kindergarten (Unedited)
Ms. Robertson

When it snows I like ot ride my 4-welr. I like to build a snowman and have a snowball fite. – *Jordan H.*

When it snows I lik to make a snow man. I like to hav snow bol fits. – *Alex C.*

When it snows I lik to play with my brthr. – *Jordyn P.*

When it snows I am going to have a snowbol fit. – *Jackson H.*

When it snows I like to mac a snobol frt. – *Cooper C.*

When it snows I like to mak a snowman. – *Jalliyah H.*

When it snows I like to drink hot coao beside the fire. – *Allison K.*

When it snows I like to build a snowman. When it snows I like to have a snowball fight. After I play I go inside and drink hot coca. – *Dylan B.*

When it snows I like to go snowbording and bild a snowball. – *Nazig D.*

When it snows I like to build a snowman. – *Raeleigh K.*

When it snows I like to play and have sum fun. – *Kelyse W.*

Wen it snohw I like to make snewgballs and make snow anjls. – *Alivia M.*

When it snoas I like to go put no my snowboots, my warm jacket and my warm glvs. – *Shea H.*

When it snows I like to have a snowball fight. I like to build snawmen. I will drenk hot coco. – *Briuna E.*

Kindergarten (Unedited)
Ms. L. O'Quinn

My family likes to go out to eat. – *Lisa B.*

My family likes to play games with me. – *Devin C.*

My famile likes to wach TV. – *Devin K.*

My family likes to go to the movies. – *Shelby N.*

My family likes to play the Wii. – *Haley C.*

My fumily likes to play wit me. – *Nyjia T.*

My mommy likes to get penny and nickels. – *Hunter B.*

My family likes to paly my Wii. – *Michael W.*

My family likes to go to slep. – *Sara M.*

My family likes to play games. – *Donovan N.*

My family likes to slep. – *Owen Y.*

My family lik to go out to et. – *Halee M.*

My family likes to go play Wii. – *Sebastian S.*

My fmilyi likes to play Sonic Tenes. – *Aaron M.*

My family likes to play the Wii. – *Annabelle H.*

Kindergarten (Unedited)
Ms. Bahnsen

I love to play games on the computer. We eat pizza with juice. I watch TV and fix puzzle pieces. – ***Benjamin N.***

I play in the snow and I mayd a snowman. Its snowing. The snow is cold. I thru a snowball. – ***Hannah S.***

I have a horse. He is a pant. His name is Skip. He lives in a born. I like to go on a trel rid wif Skip. I fil hape to have him. – ***Ellington L.***

I am good at football because I can cech the football and I can mac a tuchdaln and I can run fast and I can tacl the uthr pepl. – ***Devin H.***

I went on a trip with my dad. We went walking on a mountain in the snow. It was cold but I had fun. – ***Eymbrie P.***

I like to ride my Jeep! My Jeep has a rill radeeo. I like to drive it. – ***Olivia A.***

What I see in the sky: I can see a plane. I can see a bird. I can see a cloud. – ***Colin L.***

A girl is getting an apple. The girl got an apple. She bit the apple. The apple is good. – *Zebedee J*

The girl is getting a banana. The girl peels her banana. The girl ate the banana. The girl is throwing her mess away. – *Emma W.*

My goal is to play tennis. – *Amberli N.*

In the winter I can build a snow man. I also throw snow balls.

Chapter 2
All About Me

All About Me
Stephen T.
Ms. Winsor, 1st Grade

Do you want to know all about me? My name is Stephen. I have a mom and a dad and a sister. I like broccoli. I dislike sauce on my chicken. Things I'm good at are basketball and baseball. When I grow up I want to be a cop. That is all about me.

All About Me
Jayda R.
Ms. Winsor, 1st Grade

Do you want to know all about me? My name is Jayda R. I have a brother named Jacob that is wild. I have a mom that is beautiful and a dad that is silly. I have a dog named Bosgo that is sweet and a cat named Sheldin that is sweet. I'm good at Rummy game. When I grow up I want to be a doctor. That is all about me.

All About Me
Emmet L.
Ms. Winsor, 1st Grade

Do you want to know about me? My name is Emmet L. I like with my mom, dad, and my brother. I like ice cream. I dislike lima beans. Things I'm good at are playing and baseball. When I grow up I want to make a video game. That is all about me.

All About Me
Kyndal K.
Ms. Winsor, 1st Grade

Do you want to know all about me? My name is Kyndal K. In my family I have a mommy, a daddy, a sister named Kelbi, and a dog named Dog. I love my mommy and daddy. I like ducks. I dislike tapping. When I grow up I want to be a coach. That is all about me.

All About Me
Grace K.
Ms. Winsor, 1st Grade

Do you want to know all about me? My name is Grace K. I like pizza and ice cream and spaghetti. I am six years old. I can go to Afterschool. I like cookies and I like lunch. I do not like headaches.

All About Me
Chaeli H.
Ms. Winsor, 1st Grade

Do you want to know all about me? My name is Chaeli H. I have two brothers and a baby sister named Braelin. I have three dogs named Jackson, Molly, and Teton. I like softball. I don't like being hit and when my dog died. My mom thinks I am good at cooking. I want to be with an ambulance. That is all about me.

All About Me
Hailey H.
Ms. Winsor, 1st Grade

Do you want to know all about me? My name is Hailey H. I love my dad. I love my mom. I love my brother and I love my sister. I like apples. My least favorite food is broccoli. When I grow up I want to be a doctor. That is all about me.

All About Me
Kaylee G.
Ms. Winsor, 1st Grade

Do you want to know all about me? My mommy is very beautiful. My daddy is handsome. My sister is beautiful. My brothers are handsome. I like to read and I like ice cream. I dislike broccoli. I am good at riding two-wheelers. When I grow up I want to be a horse rider. That is all about me.

All About Me
Tyler G.
Ms. Winsor, 1st Grade

Do you want to know all about me? My name is Tyler G. I love my mom and my dad. I like rain and cars. I dislike chicken. When I grow up I want to be a Hess gas station worker. That is all about me.

All About Me
Ethan G.
Ms. Winsor, 1st Grade

Do you want to know all about me? My name is Ethan G. I have a nice family named Casey and Grace and Scott and Alley. I have a buggy sister named Grace. I like chicken and ice cream and fries. I'm good at baseball. When I grow up I want to be a professional baseball player. That is all about me.

My Favorite Foods
Mason N.
Ms. Ryan, 3rd Grade

My name is Mason and I have three favorite foods. They are brownies, ribs, and apples. I like many different foods but those are my three favorite.

My favorite dessert is brownies. I will eath them dry or chewy. They're good to me either way. I think that homemade brownies are the best with no nuts.

My favorite dinner is ribs, especially my Grandpa's ribs. He makes a special sauce that he puts on the ribs and makes them taste really good. He has a special recipe but only he and I know it. I really like ribs with a bunch of meat on them but if they're burnt, I won't eat them.

My favorite fruit is apples. I like apple because the juice runs down my face. Sweet or tart, either way, they're good to me. I like the peeling on the apple.

I enjoy lots of different foods but brownies, ribs, and apples are my favorite. What are yours?

My Life
Jesse M.
Ms. Hurndon, 3rd Grade

Hi, my name is Jesse M. I was born on February 1, 2001 at 4:58 in the morning on a rainy day in Atlanta, Georgia at Atlanta Medical Center. I was ten pounds and very long. My whole family was there to watch it all happen.

Now I am going to tell you about my wonderful family. I have two sisters named Shelby and Amber. My loving parent's names are Beth and Jim Mince and I can't forget my awesome pets Max, Daisy, Cooper, and Sam.

Now that's enough about my family facts, let's move on to learn more about my hobbies and interests. My favorite sport is baseball and my favorite food is pizza. My best subject in school is reading. I love to read. I also like to play video games, watch television, and jump on the trampoline in my free time.

The most important event that has happened to me is when I got my first puppy, Daisy. This was a special to me because I love dogs. I also always wanted a puppy.

This is My Wild Life
Shayne M.
Ms. Hurndon, 3rd Grade

Come on the train to see my life. I came in this cool world on October 16, 2001. My Mom, Dad, the nurses, and the doctor were there when I was born. I was born at Bibbs County Hospital. I weighed seven pounds and I was 17 inches long.

It is time to take a mean ride through the M. House. My parent's names are Rolando and Brandy. I have two sisters named Sierra and Shian. My brother's names are Alex and Dalen. I have some cool pets named Lilly and Junior. We have a lot of people who live in our house with us. Their names are Chopo, Litzy, Maria, Rebecca, Cynthia, and Oswaldo.

Jump on the train now to learn about my hobbies and interests. My favorite subject in school is math. I love math because it exercises my brain. Pizza is my favorite thing to eat and I also really like mashed potatoes. I also like to play on my Play Station 2 because it exercises my fingers. My favorite sports are baseball and swimming because they both exercise my legs and arms.

Now it is time for you to take a look at an important event in my life. My step mom is having a baby! My family is excited. We are going to move in a few weeks. Thanks for riding the train.

My Life
Aaron H.
Ms. Hurndon, 3rd Grade

Do you want to learn all about me? Well, if you do then hop into my head. I was born at Rockdale Hospital. I weighed 6.9 pounds and I was 19 inches long. My whole family was there to see me on my first day.

Now it is time to learn about my weird family. My sister's name is Rose and boy is she lazy. My brother is a brat and his name is Clay. I have dogs that are also lazy like my sister and my cats are very loving. I have a wonderful mother, also!

Okay, now it is time to learn about my hobbies. I love to play my Nintendo DS. My favorite foods are pizza and macaroni and cheese. I love baseball and football. I really like to play outside in my free time.

I have some wacky events that have happened in my lifetime. One is when I got my pets. My other event was when I passed 2nd grade.

My Life
Chantel J.
Ms. Hurndon, 3rd Grade

Hi, my name is Chantel and you are about to learn a lot about me so get ready. I came into this world on August 14, 2000. I was born at Southern Regional Hospital. I weighed seven pounds. Can you believe my whole family was there? Well, they were. I love my family. I have a wonderful mother, Ernestine, who is a truck driver. My dad, Wendell, is a truck driver, too. I have two brothers named Alex and Cornelius and I like to play with them all of the time.

Now I am going to tell you some of my favorite things in life. I love food and sports. I like to jump rope and ride my bike. Both of those are good exercise for you legs. My favorite sport is softball. In school I love reading. I love to act like certain characters from my books. My favorite foods are spaghetti and pizza.

I am going to tell you an important thing that has happened to me in my life. I am making good grades this year. You might ask why this is important. Well if I make good grades in school, I can go further and why should I go far because life is important!

My Parents
Cassie E.
Ms. Armstrong, 4th Grade

There are many people that I admire, but I admire my mom and dad the most. My dad Shane is so amazing. He plays fun games with me. He is also very caring. When I feel sad or lonely, he finds a way to make me smile. He can tell some funny jokes sometimes. My dad is the best.

My mother Shannon is wonderful. She cracks me up whenever I need a laugh. This makes me feel better when I am sick. My mom is a good cook. She makes the best spaghetti and meatballs. She is smart too because she is able to help me complete my homework. My mom is so awesome.

So as you can see, I have two great parents! I am very grateful to have them in my life.

Best Friends
Savannah E.
Ms. Armstrong, 4th Grade

I am the happiest girl in the world. That's because I have
two great friends. They are Katlyn and Dalyn.

We are just like sisters without the fighting part. We
attended the same school and are in the same class. We do cool
things together as well. We play games, sit together at lunch
time, and read cool books. Dalyn and Katlyn and I also like
the same kind of books and movies. It is great to have things in
common.

I love having the best two friends in the world.

Favorite Foods
Alexus E.
Ms. French, 5th Grade

Do you just crave some foods? I dream about three certain
foods! I think Sour Punch Straws are the most delightful candy
in the world. Chinese Puffs are another and they make me feel
like royalty. Last, but certainly not least, crab legs are delicious
dipped in warm, melted butter. I especially adore these three
spectacular foods.

Sour Punch Straws are the most delectable candy in this
galaxy. I love how Sour Punch Straws are so sour they make
you want to scream. My favorite flavor of Sour Punch Straws
are the green ones because they taste divine. I love it when
my daddy buys them for me at the Texaco station. Sour Punch
Straws make my day complete.

Chinese Puffs are something that I will never, ever get
tired of. I love the Chinese Puffs at the Chinese buffets. I love
how creamy they are in the middle. When they are fried, I'm in
Heaven.

Lastly, crab legs are the best seafood meat I've ever eaten.
Crab legs are delicious dipped in warm, melted butter! If you
get them from Red Lobster, you will be able to fly. I love
cracking the legs with a nutcracker. Just the sound makes my
taste buds scream.

When I want to take a little trip to Heaven I eat my favorite
foods. Sour Punch Straws make me pucker my lips. Chinese
Puffs are a Chinese wonder. I'm also sure crab legs can't be
better. I love my favorite foods. Let's eat!

Georgia X-Games Champion
Tyler J.
Mr. Griffis, 5th Grade

I don't think my mom and dad will ever be more proud of me than when I became the Georgia X-Games champion.

When I was eight years old, my team in hockey was so good that we were invited to state X-Games. We had to drive to Atlanta for hours straight from 3:00 am to 8:00 am. We were nervous because we came two years ago and we lost to the very team we were playing-The Crusaders. They had gotten new players but we got better. Nobody knew the turn out. They couldn't even imagine!

We were hoping to show them up but we were just as good as them. The first goal was scored by the Crusaders. It was 1-0 Crusaders. After that we scored four more points and they scored one more point. We won 4-2. The Hurricanes won and we were the Hurricanes.

We had a big party after we were initiated into the Georgia X-Games Hall of Fame. I loved my experience in the X-Games. That is why this will always be one of the proudest moments in my life.

Chapter 3
Our Pets

I Wish I had a Cat
Benjamin C.
Ms. Hall, 1st Grade

If I had a cat I would play with him and he would play with me. We would play together. We would play, play, play! I just wish I had a cat. I wish I had a cat for my birthday or Christmas.

My Dogs
Madison K.
Ms. Richter, 1st Grade

I have dogs. Their names are Duke and Princess and Roxie. My dogs are the best. My dogs are allergic to chocolate. My dogs do not swim. Every time people come to my house the dogs have to go in my sister's room. My dogs like to play with me. And I love my dogs.

My Dog Zoe
Abbey M.
Ms. Consolie, 2nd Grade

I love my dog Zoe. She has been living a long time and I am happy. Her birthday is August 13. She is a very nice dog. We got her before I was born and I am 8 years old. I love having Zoe at the house. She is a playful dog. Zoe is a big dog and I love her very much. She loves to play. She is very friendly and nice. If I am sitting on the couch she will come bring her toy to me. We feed her, take her outside, play with her, and love her. Zoe keeps us safe.

Miracle
Jasmine A.
Ms. Consolie, 2nd Grade

My cat's name is Miracle. She is black and white. She is a good pet. She is so cute. I love my cat. At night I make her a bed on my bed. Then I put the blanket on her. I give her food and water. Miracle is special because my mom rescued her when she was a tiny kitten. She was thrown away by someone who didn't want her. We fed her and took good care of her. Now she is a happy, healthy cat. She is very loving and sweet. She lays on me sometimes. Miracle is a very playful cat.

My Cat
Tiffany C.
Ms. Consolie, 2nd Grade

My pet cat plays. It is very funny. One day I came home and the cat was jumping on the bed. When I went into the room and sat down he was doing back flips. It was time to go to sleep and he jumped on the bed and talked to me. I put him outside but he opened the door. The next morning he was watching TV. Later he went and swam in the pool. He got out and read a book and he was back to normal. Then he went outside and climbed a tree. The end.

My Pet
Zaida M.
Ms. Lawrence, 2nd Grade

I have a pet already. He is a white, fluffy bunny. I got him from the Henry County Fair. His ears are tall and pink. He is very pretty and sweet. He is very small but sweet and soft, too. I have to get his poop up every day after school. I also have to feed him and give him water.

My Pet
Blake S.
Ms. Lawrence, 2nd Grade

If I could have any pet, it would be a baby tiger. I would name my tiger Simba. I would give him a bath and brush his hair every day. I would play games with Simba every day after school. We would eat dinner together every night. I would let Simba sleep in my bed with me all the time. Simba and I would be best friends forever!

My Pet
Josh D.
Ms. Lawrence, 2nd Grade

If I could have a pet it would be a puppy. I would name it Happy because it is a puppy. I want the puppy because it is so small and so soft and they have tiny ears and small paws. I want the puppy because it is so cute. I'm responsible and I can feed it. They're so fluffy. I can walk it every day. I can bring it to the park. I can take it to see his friends. I can take it to the fair.

My Pet
Kyle M.
Ms. Lawrence, 2nd Grade

If I could have any animal for a pet I would pick an African Grey Parrot. The African Grey usually attaches to one owner, so I would need to get a bird when it is very young. They are good talkers and I could teach it words and sayings. One African Grey needs a strong cage about 3 feet by 3 feet by 2 feet. It has to be in a vented room at around 70 degrees. I would have to feed and water the bird every day. The cage would need cleaning every week. It also needs medicine every month to keep it fit and well.

My Pet
Logan R.
Ms. Lawrence, 2nd Grade

My pet would be a dinosaur. He weighs 100 pounds. I feed him dinosaur food. I like to play with him. I like him very much. His name is Drake. I show him to my friends.

My Dog
JD M.
Ms. Ryan, 3rd Grade

I love my dog. He is good and cool. We can play and beat up some dogs and cats. His name is Blake. He is gray. He goes outside and plays with me. He is good and he won't hurt me. I love him. I think he is pretty. He loves my mom, dad, and sister. I think he is great. I love Blake.

My Little Kitten
Daniel T.
Ms. Scarbrough, 3rd Grade

I have a kitten. Its black and white and a big one. It does not like to eat a lot. It is trained to stay in the house.

My Pets
Samantha S.
Ms. Scarbrough, 3rd Grade

I've had a lot of pets. Most of them were dogs, but not all of them. I've had cats and fish too. So I guess it's not all about dogs. My pets names are Tubby, Rusty, Sarah, Nemo, T-Bone, Pepey, Mikey, Piglit, and Christian. Rusty was the best dog ever. I loved him too. Rusty died because he was very sick. I'm still sad but I know he's in a better place. Rusty was mixed with Golden Retriever and lab. I got Rusty for my 6th birthday.

Sasha was my old English Bulldog. She was one year old when my mom got her. I was not born yet. She was the cutest bulldog. We had to give her to our neighbors because she was destroying our house but we loved her. We did get to still see her. Then she died.

T-Bone is my wienerdog. He will peepee on you if you are new. Like a month ago we could not find him. One of our neighbors had a wienerdog and the coyotes killed him. We had to get Mr. Chris and found him.

Mikey and Pepey are Jack Russels so they are very hyper. Well Pepey is. She could play ball all day. Mikey is calm. He bites though. Mikey isn't nearly as hyper as Pepey.

Last but not least, Tubby. He is another bulldog. I still have him. He loves his toys. I love him. Also I love my other animals.

That's all my pets!

My Dog Coco
Parker C.
Ms. Murdock, 3rd Grade

The second dog I got was named Coco. She used to bark a lot because she was pregnant. She had four babies. Their names were Laser, Shadow, Louie, and Pebbles. We sold the puppies to people we didn't know. Coco loved to play with the puppies. Coco is very nice and doesn't like to go to the doctor. One day she went to the doctor and got a purple elephant. It's her favorite toy. We named it Fluffy.

Coco loves to lick feet, especially when you're asleep. She likes my mother the most because she is the only other girl in the family. Coco likes to stay with my mom. That's my dog Coco.

Ben
Bryce R.
Ms. Hurndon, 3rd Grade

I remember when we got our dog Ben. My granddaddy found out there was a beagle in Decatur, Georgia for sale. He cost $100. Austin, my brother, and I took turns holding Ben the whole way home.

Ben is black, white, and brown. He has freckles on his chest. He probably weighs about one hundred pounds! I can't even pick him up! He loves people to scratch his belly. He runs very, very fast. One time Ben ran off. We looked for Ben everywhere. My mom drove through subdivisions looking for him. Finally, my mom found him at the pound.

Ben is now about four years old. We have had Ben since 2005. He loves to chew bones and go for walks. That is all about my dog Ben.

Our Class Pet
Caitlynn W.
Mrs. Griffis, 5th Grade

Dear Mrs. Griffis,

For our class pet I want a hamster. They might be messy, but they are small and playful. There are three reasons why I think we should get a hamster for our class pet.

First, hamsters are playful, but small! They would be a good pet for us, because they are very hyper. I think! If you go to the pet store just to go and look, they are always playing. Hamsters are small, so they would not take up a big part of our classroom.

Another great reason to get a hamster is that they are not noisy. Let's say we have an important test. Hamsters are not so noisy that they would disturb us. If you are teaching a lesson, don't worry, because the hamster will not interrupt you. Hamsters are very quiet, depending on what they are doing. For example, if one was running around you would barely hear anything at all.

Finally, they are not messy animals. Clean up their scraps each day and that is all you have to do besides feeding him or her. For one of our jobs in class, we can switch out taking care of him. Maybe if he or she has a cage with bars that have space in between them, there may be some scraps on the floor. However, that is easy. All we have to do is sweep them up with the broom.

If you are wondering what you should get for a class pet, I personally would love a hamster to be our class pet! Also, if you are afraid to get one because they are so messy and you do not want to clean up the mess, well you can assign students to do that chore. That is why we should have a hamster or two as our class pet.

Love,
Caitlynn

My Dog Bella
Craig S.
Mrs. Partain, 4th Grade

We adopted a dog. Back then she was called Lavender Girl, but when she came home with us, we named her Bella. We didn't name her after Bella in New Moon though. We got her before there was the movie.

About a year ago, she saw her first snow. My pool was frozen, and she walked on it. I got to get her off.

We have a cat named Felix, and Bella just loves him. They like to play tag together. Felix is two years old. Everyone in the house loves her, but you better keep your door closed!

My Pets
Savannah M.
Ms. Armstrong, 4th Grade

Dear Ms. Armstrong,

I want to tell you about some special pets. I have three pets. Their names are Emma, Tuss, Madi, Izzie, Gracie, Selena. One of them died and one is missing.

Emma is very sweet. She came from the Publix parking lot. She was the last one left and my friend knew that my birthday was coming up so she paid $1.00 for her and gave her to me.　　　　That was sweet.

Tuss came from the Water Authority. They were feeding him when they decided that it was time that someone took him home because he was about to be sent to the pound. So, my dad brought him home.

Madi was put down January 9, 2001, the day before my mother's birthday. She cried all day long. It was a very sad time. Izzie is another dog. She is very hyper and loves to play. My dad said, "Izzie needs to go live with Alan and Jordan at their house." We all agreed. We did not have time to play with her. She now lives with them.

Gracie is a very sweet Pekinese. She loves to play. She is like my wake up call. If I don't get up on time she practically nibbles on my ears and nose. Selena is technically my can. She is a stray and lives in my neighbor's garage at times but in November of 2009 she went missing.

Well that was my story about the wonderful pets that are in my life and that I lost.

Oreo (Thunder Thighs)
Mikayla D.
Ms. Elmer, 4th Grade

Cats are crazy and wacko. There are also plain and ordinary cats. My cat Oreo is plain, weird, fat, lazy, and fluffy. He weighs about fourteen pounds, but I can't tell; he keeps on wiggling. He sits on the couch, on my bed, or the floor all day long. His name is Oreo because he is black and white. We also call him Thunder Thighs.

One day when I went home, I went in through the front door. When my mom told me to let the dogs and cats out, I went to the garage door. When I opened the door, Oreo had a dead bird in front of him. I was happy and sad. Oreo did the right thing. He knew I was coming, and he couldn't speak because he's a cat. Instead, he brought the bird to me. He didn't kill the bird. The garage door hit the bird, and Oreo picked it up.

Puppy Survivor
Samantha K.
Mrs. Griffis, 5th Grade

I am so happy to be able to tell the story of the puppy survivor. When she was born, she was born to a very young mother. The mother was so young that she did not know how to take care of her puppies. When the puppy survivor was born, there was another puppy also.

Both of the puppies were outside with the mommy. My sister went to check on them, and they were fine. It was when she went out a couple of hours later that we realized something was wrong. This is when she saw the black puppy lying there not breathing. She rushed inside to tell my dad. He said we would need to help take care of the other puppy to make sure it survived.

With only one puppy left, we knew we had to take special care of it if we wanted a healthy puppy. We fed her, kept her warm, and made sure she had everything she needed. Now she is a month old. She is eating big dog food. She loves to play tug a war on your pants and chase you all around. I am so happy I have the story of the puppy survivor to tell with you. As she continues to grow and explore, I am sure I will have many more stories to share!

Chapter 4
Holidays and Trips

The Fall Festival
Kyle D.
Ms. Hall, 1st Grade

I went to the Fall Festival. I gobbled up a cookie. I rode a black pony. Ms. Blount was there. I ate red candy. I played games.

My Christmas Tree
Makayla B.
Ms. Hall, 1st Grade

My tree is pretty. It has ornaments and an angel. It is pretty.

Going to the Mountains
Dylan P.
Ms. Hall, 1st Grade

I am so excited! I am going to the mountains this weekend! It is awesome. I am going to hunt bears there. In the cabin there's buffalo skin on the wall. It is humongous! You should see it. My dad's friend shot it and a skunk skin too.

My Christmas
Chase M.
Ms. Richter, 1st Grade

My Christmas was the best Christmas in the whole, wide world. It was the best. I got lots of stuff at Christmas. It was a blast.

My Trip to Florida
Anneliese C.
Ms. Brown, 1st Grade

Let me tell you about my trip to Florida. Me, my mom, dad, and two brothers went to Florida with our aunt Katie. She invited us to go with her. At Florida there is a beach. The beach had lots of shells. We went to feed birds little bread crumbs.

One night we went out and let go of fireworks. It was sunny at the beach. We saw skygliding. We tried to catch minnows but they were too fast. One time a minnow jumped and hit my little brother in the forehead. It was funny. Me and my family built sandcastles. We saw the sunset. It was cool. Now you know all about my awesome trip to Florida!

A Special Place
Lily H.
Ms. Brown, 1st Grade

Do you know about my special place I went to? Let me tell you. Me Lily, my mom Kimberly, my dad Charlie, and my sister Courtney went to White Water. It was very sunny. We rode on the Tornado but I didn't like it. My favorite one was the Play Land. We watched my dad and my sister. The last thing we did was the slide. It went really fast. Soon it was time to go. I had fun. The End.

Reindeer
Gage J.
Ms. Richter, 1st Grade

Once there was a reindeer and this evil guy. He built evil machines to make animals like donkeys that stay evil because they destroy Christmas.

The Super Bowl
Christian J.
Ms. Brown, 1st Grade

I went to the Super Bowl. Me, my sister Chrinyson, my mom Neasa, and Christina went together. When the game was over we won and we went in a limo and we drove to a restaurant. When we got there me and my teammates chased each other. When my food came out I sat down to eat. When we were done we went home. The Super Bowl was awesome!

The Farm
Riley T.
Ms. Brown, 1st Grade

We went to the farm in kindergarten. It was fun. We saw cows. We got to pick pumpkins and we went down a slide. It took us a long time to get there. I saw horses and chickens and a cow. The cow and horses were eating. We also got to pick strawberries. We went in a maze. The maze had ant beds and corn. After we came back from our field trip I said that was the best field trip ever.

Stone Mountain
Colby W.
Ms. Winsor, 1st Grade

You might want to go to Stone Mountain. It has fireworks and a mountain climbing and a train. You can hear the train's horn and you can hear the train going down the train track. Sometimes you have to wait for the big train going over the sidewalk and you can hear fireworks. And even a station where you used to buy tickets to ride the train. It's for looks.

Fall Break
Avery D.
Ms. Winsor, 1st Grade

Fall break was fun. First, my dad picked me up and drove me to the horse riding place. I was really, really happy. Next, we got out of the truck and my dad and I each got on a horse and we rode in the field. Then, my dad and I raced horses. Last, I got off the horse and I felt sad because I had to go home. That fall break was fun.

Thanksgiving Day
Brianna C.
Ms. Richter, 1st Grade

On Thanksgiving Day I ate turkey and rice. Next I played cards with my family. Next I went outside to ride my bike. I went to my room to play with my sister. I went to the store to buy cereal and milk. Next I went to bed.

On Christmas Day
Edmund H.
Ms. Richter, 1st Grade

On Christmas Day me and my family went for a present hunt all around the house and went to open our presents. Also we played Mario and Sonic at the Olympic Winter Games. Also we went to our grandma's house and ate dinner. We went shopping for some clothes. We watched tv and sat down and ate. Also we said our prayers and went to bed. In the morning I woke up and read a book and ate breakfast and played with my football men and talked.

I Believe
Cecilia B.
Ms. Kirbow, 2nd Grade

I believe in Christmas. Santa always eats my cookies and he takes the carrots to the reindeer. And he leaves presents under the Christmas tree. And sometimes I hear the bells.

I Believe
Joshua J.
Ms. Kirbow, 2nd Grade

Why I believe in Christmas is Santa brings Christmas to the world. And it's Jesus' birthday. I believe in Christmas and I believe in Santa Clause.

I Believe
Gary S.
Ms. Kirbow, 2nd Grade

I believe in Christmas because it's Jesus' birthday. And because Santa brings presents. Then one more day until my birthday and I get what I want.

I Believe
Hannah I.
Ms. Kirbow, 2nd Grade

I believe in Christmas because I believe in Santa Clause. I also believe for all the joy. But most of all Jesus.

I Believe
Mia B.
Ms. Kirbow, 2nd Grade

I believe in Christmas because Santa's real. Santa made Christmas. There must be Christmas if Santa's real. I believe in Christmas because of the presents that Santa brings. Because if you have a star on top of your Christmas tree.

I Believe
Anslie M.
Ms. Kirbow, 2nd Grade

Why I believe in Christmas is because you can get presents and because if you stop believing you stop receiving. It is also the day baby Jesus was born.

Winter Wonder Land
Kaitlyn S.
Ms. J. O'Quinn, 2nd Grade

Once I made a winter wonder land. It had red lights, green lights, blue lights, and white lights. You could hear Christmas carols all around you. There were a lot of Christmas trees. Like a candy cane tree, a jingle bell tree, a snowy tree, and a ribbon tree. Then I made a Frosty the Snowman. It was so cool. Then there were reindeer. Then at eleven o'clock we had to go so Santa would give us presents. The End!

Holiday Break
Riley M.
Ms. J. O'Quinn, 2nd Grade

On Christmas day I got some new Bakugans for Christmas. We all went to my cousin's for dinner. On New Year's eve we had fireworks. On New Year's Day my mom kept cousins until today. Yesterday I got Bakugan games for the Wii. My dad and I played the Wii all day yesterday. I beat my dad on the Wii yesterday. The End.

How the Grinch Stole my Winter Break
Brian D.
Mr. Deabenderfer, 2nd Grade

If the Grinch stole my Xbox 360 and my Game Cube I would be so mad. The Grinch lives in a cave beside my house. He hates everybody except his dog Max. The cave is dark inside. You can only see him. He is mean. Everybody does not like him. He is always red. He messes up all the streets and makes us clean it up. The Grinch hid my games and I found them. When I tried to play it and it showed the Grinch's face and it said, "Ho Ho." I was mad so I looked for them again. I found them. This time when I came back the Game Cube was gone. I found it. It was in my mom's closet. When I came back, the TV was gone but I found it in my closet. I have two Game Cubes and if they broke I would have one more left If the Grinch stole that one I would have nothing to do all day. I will have to play outside. I hope that the Grinch is in camouflage in the woods. Then the Grinch will steal the things I'm playing with and I would have to go to sleep.

How the Grinch Stole My Winter Break
Jasminelee M.
Mr. Deabenderfer, 2nd Grade

The Grinch slithered through the snow to sneak into
the house of one of Mr. D`s students. The Grinch chose my
house. The Grinch took my cat and bed away. The Grinch took
away my toys, games, perfumes, and lotion. When I woke up
Christmas morning everything was gone. The Grinch even took
all the radios, stuffed animals, and Christmas cards, Barbie
Dolls, and our Roast Beef! When I woke up Sunday morning
the flowers were gone too! The Grinch stole our new shoes,
lamps, mp3 players, Nintendos, and clothes. The Grinch is
green with red eyes.

The Grinch that Stole the Winter Break
Ian C.
Mr. Deabenderfer, 2nd Grade

There once was a Grinch that lived on Oogly-Boogly Hill.
He hates Christmas. He's only one inch tall. But when he sees
or hears anything or anybody he hates, he'll grow a whopping
ten feet! He also has a (the next word I will spell wrong on
purpose because this creature is so sad) Raindeer. In fact, he
has nine (each a brother or sister to Santa's Reindeer.) There're
theories like his eyes are to small so he couldn't see the true
meaning of Christmas. Now, I lived at the bottom of the
hill. So when Christmas was about a week away, each night,
the Grinch would use his magic powers to steal a day. But,
Wednesday afternoon, I went up the hill to drive the Grinch out
of town (with a machete!) My parents were so proud of me,
they gave me five early Christmas presents. Here are the things
my family would have done on the days the Grinch magically
stole: On Friday, the 18th of December, I would've gone to
school if the Grinch hadn't stolen Friday. On Saturday, the
19th of December, I would've gone hiking in South Carolina
if the Grinch hadn't stolen Saturday. On Sunday, the 20th of
December, I would've gone to a Falcon's game, if the Grinch
hadn't stolen Sunday. On Monday, December 21st, I would've
gone fishing, if the Grinch hadn't stolen Monday. On Tuesday,

December 22nd, I would've gone skiing in Colorado, if the Grinch hadn't stolen Tuesday.

Now here are the things I got for Christmas: A pack of 20 HG Baseball cards, a DS game called Fossil Fighters, 4 Lego sets, 2 packs of Star Wars figures, a game of Chess, and a Red Rider BB gun (just kidding about the BB gun). Here are the things I did after Christmas: On Saturday December 26th I visited my great-grandmother's house to get more presents. On Sunday, December 27th, I went to the movies to see A Christmas Carole with my friend, Zack B. On Monday, December 28th, I went to St. Louis, Missouri to get MORE Christmas presents. On Tuesday, December 29th, (for some reason) I went to the Beach (just joking around. Ha Hah Ha!) On Wednesday, December 30th, I went to Florida to spend one night. On Thursday, December 31st, I went to my grandmother's house to get even MORE Christmas presents. On Friday, January 1st (2010), I went to my other grandmother's for New Year's Eve and New Year's Day. On Saturday, January 2nd, I had a New Year's Day party at my grandmother's house. Finally, I'm almost done writing this story. And on Tuesday, I... went back to school (in a new year.2010!) Anyway, I sure hope the other stories are better than mine. Anyway, MERRY CHRISTMAS!!!

The End

(P.S. I was lying about my parents being proud of me. They were so mad, they grounded me till Christmas Day. Also, on Sunday, I set out to find the Grinch and to teach him the true meaning of Christmas and to bring him back.) NOW, we can end this story.

THE END
(P.S. I...) Don't worry. I'm just joking around again. Ha hah ha!!!

How the Grinch Stole my Winter Break
Courtney B.
Mr. Deabenderfer, 2nd Grade

If the Grinch stole my winter break, I would feel sad and mad. If the Grinch stole the snow we couldn't play in it and feel sad. If the Grinch stole my presents and stockings I would feel sad and we can't get what we wanted for Christmas. If the Grinch stole our food we would have nothing to eat. We would have to go back to school if the Grinch stole my winter break and I would feel mad because I would have no winter break for Christmas. But the Grinch stole everything in my house at night. And when he finished my house which was the last one the Grinch made me do lots of work that night. The Grinch made me sweep, do dishes, and other stuff while he sat down and had fun. I had to do trashcans, his homework; even he made me clean the toilets. He even made me clean the fishbowl. Feeding the fish was still fun. He made me clean the driveway and made me clean the windows while he sat down and ate cherries. It was exhausting. But at the end his heart grew 6 sizes that day and he gave everything back. He even said sorry for making me do work. I said it's ok. At least the house is clean I said.

The Grinch that Stole my Winter Break
Nolan C.
Mr. Deabenderfer, 2nd Grade

There was a Grinch that lived on a snowy mountain. He was trying to steal Christmas, but did not work. He took everything. He took my TV, dresser, desk, TV stand, Lego box, action figures box, and last but not least the Christmas tree. He even took my brother's stuff and my mom and dad's stuff. He stole our food and our dog's. HE TOOK EVERYTHING!

Then he went to the next house and the next and the next and the next and the next, but last but not least THE VERY LAST HOUSE! Before the Grinch came to our house the Grinch made a ship that blows out fire. After the Grinch stole everybody's stuff he did not give our stuff back.

Then the Grinch made us clean the walls. Then the Grinch made us clean the floors, then the tables. The Grinch made us clean the inside of the desks then the top and the bars and then the bottom. Then the Grinch made us pull the sled up the hill.

Then the Grinch made the teachers come back to school to teach us. The Grinch stole my clothes, my shoes, my socks, my pants, my shorts, my gloves, and my hats. The Grinch stole my vacation. The Grinch has on a Santa Claus hat, gloves, pants, boots, and shirt. The Grinch never gave back the vacation he stole. The Grinch made us be his helpers to steal people's vacations.

How the Grinch Stole my Winter Break
Kaylee S.
Mr. Deabenderfer, 2nd Grade

Once upon a time there was a Grinch. The Grinch was evil. The Grinch stole my holiday. The Grinch is meaner then you think. He took my games. Then he sent me to school. I said, "He was stupid."

He took my Wii because I said he was stupid. I told him, "Why can't you give me a break."

The Grinch responded, "Fine! I will give you one day off."

I replied, "Hey why can't you play videogames with me?" He was nice when I said videogames. Then we became friends. We agreed to play on the Wii. We played Wii Resort. The Grinch gave us a chocolate bar. He also gave us chocolate milk. We played all day long until we were tired. Then mom called him to babysit me.

"Want to read?" I said.

"Sure! Why not?" he said.

We read all night long. We were best friends forever.

The Grinch that Stole My Winter Break
Sara G.
Mr. Deabenderfer, 2nd Grade

The Grinch hates Christmas. He is mean. He is green. He is tall. The Grinch's eyes are red. The Grinch got in a fight with me.

Once there was a Grinch that lived next door in a cave, he came over and stole my bike. He will steal my TV because he is so mean. He even stole my Christmas presents. He likes to steal stuff. One day, he went to my friend's house and stole her bed. My friend sleeps on the floor now. My friend tried to stop it but we wouldn't stop it from happening. Then we stopped the Grinch because my friend yelled, "Stop!" The Grinch ran off after he dropped my stuff.

Later on that day, we ran over to the cave. The Grinch yelled, "Get away!"

My friend and I ran out of the cave and back to our house.

I asked, "Will you give me a break? The Grinch might steal my fun."

The Grinch responded, "Sure come play video games with me."

"OK. Can we play Puppy Island?" I say.

"Sure, Come on."

We run to the house faster than you never have. "Can we play Wii Fit after that?"

" Sure." Finally we're there.

"Come in."

"Please sit."

"Let me turn it on. It's on now."

"Can I go first?'

"Guests go first."

"Alright. Can we Wii Fit first?"

"Sure. Anyways I haven't put in the disk yet. "

"Let me get the board out."

"I'll get it out for you. Thanks bud. "

"You are welcome. "

"No problem. Step on the board. "

"Hit favorites."

"Hit tight rope."

"Keep your balance. I am. Lean to the right. "

"Lean to the left."
"Jump!"
"You made it. Wahoo!" (Celebrating)
"Here's you price. Thank you. "
"No problem. It's time for me to leave. "
"You can stay for dinner."
"Come in the kitchen."
"What are we eating? Soft tacos. Cool. "
"Yep, especially with beef and cheese."
"Yep. Let's eat."
"This is cool. Yep these are good. Thank you."
"No problem. "
"Well it's time for me to go home."

The Grinch Stole My Winter Break.
Kaitlyn H.
Mr. Deabenderfer

The Grinch said, "I will steal your winter break," and he did. He stole two whole weeks of my vacation. Now I have to go to school. And now I have to go to work. The Grinch stole my winter break. The Grinch made me wash his feet and the Grinch made me give him a bath. The Grinch made me feed him some green beans. The Grinch said go get me some socks, so I did. The Grinch said, "If you don't work for me you will go to school on the weekend." The Grinch wants to take all my vacation. The Grinch is bossy. The Grinch has me doing all the work. Christmas is coming up. He is going to make me go to school on Christmas and I will have to get him a present. The Grinch made me sing his favorite song. The Grinch is mean and bossy. Nobody likes the Grinch. He made me run a bath. He made me get him a bar of soap and a towel. I'm getting bossed around. The Grinch said, "I don't care if you are tired. Get to work. If you don't you will work for me for the rest of your life." The Grinch is a rude nasty slob. The Grinch wants Chinese food. Now I know he is lazy. I want to know why he is so lazy, so he asked for a fork. So I got him one.

How the Grinch Stole my Winter Break
Keion V.
Mr. Deabenderfer, 2nd Grade

It was the last day before Christmas break. We were drinking soda and eating our cake. Keeli was coming to my house so we could play. Momma and Daddy were on their way. There was nothing that could ruin this day.

We heard a message on the radio station; that the Grinch wanted to take our Christmas vacation. Then the classroom got as quiet as a mouse, and I yelled, "I want to go to grandma's house." Mr. D. called the principal to see if he could fix it.

The principal said, "I'll give the Grinch two tickets to the beach." If I give him the tickets now it won't be too late and we all can still enjoy our Christmas break.

So the Grinch took the tickets and said thank you and yelled, "I will see you after the Christmas break."

How the Grinch Stole my Winter Break
Lauren H.
Mr. Deabenderfer, 2nd Grade

Once upon a time there was a Grinch that hated Christmas and lived on a mountain. A girl lived at the bottom of the mountain and her name was Lauren. Every day she looked out her window and looked up to the top of the mountain and wondered if the Grinch would come down. One night the Grinch scared Lauren. When she screams the Grinch goes back to the mountain. On Christmas night the Grinch saw Santa Clause leaving. He went to the people's house and took their presents. The Grinch took everything, even the firewood. He came to the last house on the street. It was Lauren's house. He went down the chimney and got stuck. When he got out, he took everything but the Christmas tree. The Grinch was going to stuff up the tree but he heard a peep sound and turned around and hid behind the couch.

Lauren said, "Why are you going to take our Christmas tree?"

42

You know the Grinch. He was sneaky. He made up an awful lie and said, "Darling, what do you need? I'm taking it to give it water."

Lauren said, "Do you know the Grinch? People think he is mean, but I know he's nice inside. He's green and lives at the top of the mountain." The fake Santa Clause gave her some orange juice and sent her to bed. Then he stuffed up the tree. While Lauren slept the Grinch took everything. He left only a crumb, even too small for a mouse. The Grinch's sleigh broke down because it was too heavy to carry the presents up the mountain. Max, his dog tried to carry him up with everything almost coming off the sleigh. Max was tired of carrying the presents, Christmas tree, and turkeys.

Mr. Grinch said to Max, "Why did you stop? Keep going!" But Max just laid there and did nothing. In the morning the mayor of the town said, "Who did this and why?"

Then Lauren looked up at the tip top of the mountain and said, "Christmas is still here, it doesn't matter if our presents and trees and turkeys are gone. I am happy that our stuff is gone because he couldn't take our feelings." Lauren left to go to the Grinch's house. There was a tunnel so you can get to the Grinch's house. Lauren saw all the presents, Max and the Grinch on the side of the mountain. She thought he was going to fall, so she helped him get to a safe place. The Grinch's heart grew because she wasn't mad at him for taking the presents.

The Grinch took all the presents back to the town and said, "Let's feast." The Grinch cut the turkey and they passed it down the table. Everybody cheered because he brought the Christmas stuff back.

The Grinch That Stole My Winter Break
Patrick H.
Mr. Deabenderfer, 2nd Grade

My family lived in the mountains and there was a Grinch on top of the mountain. He was green and 5 feet tall. He did not like Christmas. One day the Grinch and I got in a fight.

That Christmas he got a sleigh and then he made a Santa hat and a Santa suit. He did not have a reindeer. The Grinch had

2 antlers on a board. He looked at Max, his dog, and he thought that Max could be his reindeer. He tied the antler to Max's head. He tied a rope to the sleigh and to Max's collar. And then they went down the mountain to my house. He went down the chimney and he got stuck for a few seconds then he dropped in my living room. He stole our town on a table in the house. The Grinch stole our fire wood. Then he stole our presents from Santa. Then the Grinch put all the stuff that he had and put it in a bag and stuffed it up the chimney and outside to Max. He got a cane and shot all the spheres in a hole in the corner. Then he took our Christmas tree. When I woke up that night and got out of my bed and went down stairs to get a drink the Grinch was there. He was stuffing the Christmas tree up the chimney. I asked, "What are you doing to our Christmas tree?"

The Grinch said, "There were some lights that would not light on your tree." He was taking it back to his shop to fix the lights. I went back to bed and fell back asleep. The Grinch took our presents and he took our wreathes and our blowup snow man. Then he took the other people's decorations.

Then in the morning all the little and big children had to go to school. At school some of the children cleaned the school halls. Some of the children cleaned the classrooms. Then they picked up the trash outside on the playground. Then they cleaned the walls. They cleaned the doors. Then they cleaned the computer area. Then they went home. And then the Grinch returned all the decorations and presents.

How the Grinch Stole my Winter Break
Shelton C.
Mr. Deabenderfer, 2nd Grade

The Grinch came to my house and I thought it was Santa Claus. He had red eyes and weird fingers. He had a weird neck. He had a small heart and small shoes. He had yellow around his eyes. He had long hair.

The Grinch took my tree because it had a busted light on it. He said he would fix it at his workshop. I figured out it was the Grinch. I shot him.

How the Grinch Stole my Winter Break
Zack B.
Mr. Deabenderfer, 2nd Grade

The Grinch will take my present. The Grinch will take my dog. The Grinch will take my tree. The Grinch will take my bike. The Grinch will take my game. The Grinch lives in the cave. The Grinch went to my house. The Grinch lives uphill in the cave. The Grinch has red eyes and big hands and big feet. The Grinch is tall. The Grinch stole my fun vacation. The Grinch made me clean my room.

How the Grinch stole my Winter Break
Miguel R.
Mr. Deabenderfer, 2nd Grade

The Grinch will steal my winter break and the Grinch was my neighbor. One day I heard him that he said that he will steal this Christmas. When it was our winter break it was almost Christmas. When it was night time we went to sleep. When it was the next day and when we saw the Christmas tree. Our presents, and everything was gone.

When I saw the Grinch going to his cave I followed him but I didn't follow him all the way because my mom was calling me. One time the Grinch told all the kids to go to school on the winter break. Our teacher was the Grinch and he was so mean.

The Grinch liked everything except Christmas. The Grinch stole Christmas and was mean because his heart was little. When we were at school the Grinch gave us a little time for everything and we didn't finish our snack or our work. The Grinch made all the days the same. The Grinch made some rules we didn't like at school and at work.

On the next day the Grinch was so sleepy that he didn't wake up. We went to play games but the Grinch stole them so we played some games that we just needed ourselves. We played some games like hide and seek, tag, and other games and we had fun. The Grinch woke up but then he slept again. The Grinch slept all day and when he was sleeping we got all the things the Grinch stole. When the Grinch woke up he saw that all the things were gone. On the next day and the others the Grinch didn't sleep he just slept when we slept. The Grinch didn't sleep because he didn't want us to steal the things. The Grinch said that we are not going to make anymore Christmas things.

The Grinch made us do different things. The Grinch had new rules and we didn't like them. In school we cannot eat things, we get a lot of home work, we don't do fun things, and we do a lot of things. When we finish going to school we go again. When we finish going to school again we give the Grinch everything he wants. When we finish giving the Grinch everything he wants we do a lot of work. We go to sleep when we finish doing our work. Every day we do the same things.

One day the Grinch was sick and on that day we didn't do the things the Grinch told us to do just take care of him. On the 5th day the Grinch didn't feel sick anymore and now we had to do the things we always do. On the other day we had a little more time to do things the Grinch told us to do. On the same day the Grinch let us go to the restroom and he let us just a little and then we went to sleep. This day was so close to Christmas but we didn't decorate for Christmas. The Grinch's heart was growing just a little bit and he was a little nice. When we were at school we just did little things that were fun. This time the Grinch made us do a little work and we ate a little more food. There were just 3 more days until Christmas and we were happy but not with our toys that we wanted. When we finished working we wanted to have some toys. The other day had passed and it was Christmas. The Grinch's heart grew big and he was nice and gave us the toys. We had a good Christmas and we sang songs and did other things.

How the Grinch Stole My Christmas Break
Tucker M.
Mr. Deabenderfer, 2nd Grade

The Grinch stole my Christmas break because he hates Christmas break. The Grinch would stop my cousin from coming. The Grinch stole my toys. The Grinch stole my DS, the snow, and the computer. The Grinch stole my books, Wii, and my games. The Grinch stole my brain. The Grinch stole my DS games, my ornaments, and my two front teeth. The Grinch has no friends.

The Grinch could kidnap my family. His heart is two sizes smaller than it is supposed to be. He is evil. Then he turned good and gave back all of the stuff. If he stole my Christmas break, I would be mad and sad. His dog Max is nice. The Grinch is mean to his dog.

He could make me clean up. He might keep the presents for Christmas. His brother is nice. He helps save Christmas. The Grinch lives next to me. The Grinch is green. His dog is brown. He might be nice. He might come to town. The Grinch might be Santa's elf. Max might be Santa's dog. Max might be a spy. His owner might be a secret Santa. He might steal Cali's and Miranda's DS and DS games. He might steal Santa's milk and cookies. He might steal 2011-3011. He might go to bullying school to learn not to steal anymore. He might steal my Christmas spirit. He might steal my friends.

His brother might give back 2011-3011. His brother is Joey. His sister is Emily. His twin sister is Tiffany. Both of hi sisters are nice. The Grinch has an Uncle Robert and Aunt Charlotte. The Grinch is very hairy. Mrs. Jennifer Grinch is also very, very mean. Mr. Grinch's name is Lee. He has $20,000,000. The Grinch sometimes burns, breaks, or sells the toys he steals. The Grinch is not nice to children. I would cry if the Grinch stole my winter break.

When I was going on vacation, the Grinch stole my tire so I couldn't go. He made me go to school instead.

The Grinch will love winter break. He will give back all the toys.

A Thanksgiving Story
Sam S.
Ms. Lawrence, 2nd Grade

One day an Indian took a walk in the woods. He saw something pretty, very, very pretty. He walked up and saw a pretty turkey! The turkey was crying. The Indian asked him why he was crying. The turkey said because he didn't have any friends. The Indian said, "I don't either." The Indian asked if the turkey wanted to be his friend. The turkey said, "Sure!" So they played together until it was dark. They said goodbye to each other. They were friends for the rest of their lives.

The Case of the Missing Turkey
Drake P.
Ms. Lawrence, 2nd Grade

My mom and I are going to make Thanksgiving dinner for our family. We put the turkey in the oven to bake. Then we started to make our side dishes and desserts. A few hours later, our turkey was done. We put everything on the table and then we discovered the turkey was missing. We looked all over and could not find the turkey. Our guests were starting to arrive hungry. Everyone wanted to know where the turkey was because they wanted to eat. We heard chopping noises under the table. We found my sister, Kaylie, feeding the dog turkey.

Pilgrims and Indians
Alex M.
Ms. Lawrence, 2nd Grade

The Pilgrims met the Indians on Thanksgiving Day. To remember this day, we celebrate a party. Indians love corn. They wait so they can eat it. Pilgrims eat turkey. Boy Pilgrims and girl Pilgrims have to wear the same clothes. Indians wear animal clothes.

My Summer Vacation
Laurel S.
Ms. Ryan, 3rd Grade

I went to the mountains with my grandparents. We went on this ride where you are in the movie theater and the chairs move. It was so fun. We went to four different hotels. They all had swimming pools. When we were in Dollywood, an ant bit me. At first I thought a bee stung me. Then I saw an ant in my shirt and knew an ant had bit me. My nana had this kind of medicine and she put it on my bug bite.

When we were there my brother and I had the best time ever. We went to High Falls water park, Six Flags, and more. After that my Nana, Papa, brother and I went to play putt-putt. My Papa didn't want to play. So he did the scores. My Nana had a 52. My brother and I tied with 51, so we won. When we were there we went to this place and it had putt-putt. It also had a ride called Earthquake. When we were first there I thought it was going to be boring but it turned out fun. We also got ice cream there. I decided that it was my second favorite place. My first is Disney World.

Finally the day came that we all didn't want to come. We had to leave. That was how my summer went at the mountains.

My New Year's Resolution
Raydon W.
Ms. Murdock, 3rd Grade

My New Year's resolution for 2010 is to make straight As. One way I will reach my goal is to try and make 100s. Another way is to try my best with my groups to make 100s. Other ways are to read in Reader's Workshop and write in Writer's Workshop. Finally I can help others and do my very best to keep my eyes on my own paper. Those are the ways I can reach my goal for the year.

New Year's Resolution
Tatum S.
Ms. Murdock, 3rd Grade

My New Year's resolution for 2010 is to make my mom and dad happy. One way is to use my manners. I won't disturb them when they're doing something. I can do more chores. They will be happy that I did that. That's ways to obey your parents.

New Year's Resolution
Jada C.
Ms. Murdock, 3rd Grade

My New Year's Day resolution for 2010 is to become organized with my time. One way is I will stay on topic in my writing and start staying on green and make better grades. I will reach my AR goal to make this a better and best year ever!

New Year's Resolution
Katie P.
Ms. Murdock, 3rd Grade

My New Year's resolution is to get plenty of sleep. Getting plenty of sleep is good. It helps you to run fast. It helps your heart beat. Finally it helps your body.

New Year's Resolution
Mackenzie S.
Ms. Murdock, 3rd Grade

My New Year's resolution for 2010 is to become better organized with my time. One of my ways is to reach my AR goals. Another way is to make better grades, 100s or 90s and up. I can use better habits like playing with the dogs and taking baths and keeping my desk clean. I have to stay on green all the time. I have to get plenty of sleep. If not, I get grumpy.

These are my ways I plan to be better organized this year.

New Year's Resolution
Tatum H.
Ms. Murdock, 3rd Grade

My New Year's resolution for 2010 is to reach my AR goal. One way I could do that is to take more AR tests. Two is read more books and then take AR tests on them. Three, go to the library more and check out more books and read them three times so I can take my AR tests on them. Finally I can read my books more than three times and that would help a lot to take an AR test and reach my goal. Those are the ways I can reach my AR goal.

New Year's Resloution
Tyler R.
Ms. Murdock, 3rd Grade

My New Year's resolution for 2010 is to keep my grades up so I can play baseball. One way I can do that is to get one hundreds. Another way is to write neater. Finally, I can study my spelling words. Those are the ways I can live up to my New Year's resolution.

New Year's Resolution
Clay B.
Ms. Murdock, 3rd Grade

My New Year's resolution for 2010 is to be better in school. One way is to make better grades. Another way is to be on green or blue. Finally, is to reach my AR goal. Those are the ways I plan to be better in school this year.

New Year's Resolution
Kyle J.
Ms. Murdock, 3rd Grade

My New Year's resolution for 2010 is to be a good student. First, I can be on track and get good grades. Second is to be orderly and good. Last, I can have a good year. Those are the ways to be a good student.

Six Flags
Jacob M.
Ms. Ryan, 3rd Grade

Last summer, I went to Six Flags with my family. I rode the Mind Bender, Bat Man, and I saw the Ninja. The Mind Bender was my favorite ride. There were lots of twists, turns, and a cork screw. It was amazing.

My second favorite ride was the Bat Man. I was stunned by all the loops. I was dazed after a while. My dad sat with my brother behind me. When we got off my little brother started crying.

My least favorite was the Ninja. I had eaten before I got on the Ninja so I didn't get to go on the ride. The bummer was I had to watch other people ride. Then all of us left.

Thunder River
Julian T.
Ms. Ryan, 3rd Grade

The ride Thunder River at Six Flags was fun. It spins around and you get all wet. I bought a hat at a store. I won a Scooby Doo tie, and a green monkey. The monkey's name is Jungle Jim. My sister got a t-shirt. I saw Batman and Joker and I got a Batman cape. My sister got a Wonder Woman cape. My mom got a Batgirl cape all by playing a game. My Dad and Grandma got nothing. I also got a stuffed Batman. My sister got a stuffed Wonder Woman. When my dad got on the scales at Six Flags it went to 30.

My Journey at Six Flags
Joel B.
Ms. Ryan, 3rd Grade

If you like fast Ferris wheels than you'll like my story. My story will be about me going to Six Flags over Georgia. When you keep reading you'll probably want to go, too.

When you're going into the line you'll see that the Ferris wheel is really called the Wheely Ride. It is red and big. The line wasn't very long though. My mom and dad went together while my brother and I went together. When we were going to go on, a man threw up in one of the red seats. We skipped that spot and went on. The workers closed all the doors and we slowly went sideways and then we went faster and faster. I could only see my brother's hair.

When I finished riding the wheely ride I was getting hungry. My dad and mom took us to the picnic area. The picnic area was big, brown, and not pretty but I didn't care because I was getting hungry. I ate hamburgers, hotdogs, and ice cream. It was good!

Summer
Avery C.
Ms. Ryan, 3rd Grade

This summer I went to Six Flags, White Water, and the beach. I rode everything except the 54" rides at Six Flags. My favorite one is the Ninja. It has flips, it goes 300 mph, and finally has 2 corkscrews.

At White Water, I rode everything except one ride. My favorite one was Cliffhanger. It goes straight down! Woooosh!

The beach was awesome. We saw a crab but we missed it with the net. I also caught a big, gray tasty fish. Mom said I saved her $36.00

I think you see I loved my summer. Make sure you visit White Water, Six Flags, and the beach.

Here We Go
McKenzie S.
Ms. Hurndon, 3rd Grade

Hi, my name is McKenzie and I would like to tell you about the time that I went to Gatlinburg, Tennessee. It is going to be a fun trip. Here is my story. When we started up the mountain my ears were popping. When you go up a mountain, your ears pop. Anyway, it was seven o'clock when we were on the top! It was really cold up there. When we got there we stayed in a hotel called The Resort. It was really nice. We rode go carts and my sister had to look over the steering wheel to see. We also played mini-golf. My step-brother and my dad tied for first, I was in second, my step-sister was in third, my little step-brother was in fourth, and my little sister was in fifth. My family went on the sky lift but my mom and I decided to stay on the ground and watch. This was a cool vacation.

Chapter 5
Narratives

The Peacock and the Stork
Ashley B.
Ms. Winsor, 1st Grade

There once was a very boastful but very beautiful peacock. He would always show off and say, "Look at me, the most beautiful bird in the world." Nobody looked at him. Only some other birds if he was that loud. Nobody stood up to him to say anything until one day… The peacock was by the pool and a stork came along.

"Good morning," said the stork.

"Whatever," said the rude peacock. For a moment they drank in silence. Then the peacock said, "You have the most ugly feathers and wings I have ever seen. So plain and white compared to mine!"

"Well, at least I can fly with them," said the stork as he flew away.

Moral: Beauty doesn't make you better and it's not what you've got, it's how you use it.

Going Outside
Lazaro M.
Ms. Hall, 1st Grade

I like to go outside because it is fun and cool. I can play tag with my mom and with my dad.

Fossils
Keith J.
Ms. Hall, 1st Grade

Yesterday I was digging a hole for my dad. He is a builder building a pool. And when I was digging a hole I found two fossils! I made a dinosaur.

Six Flags
Savannah N.
Ms. Hall, 1st Grade

If I read six hours I will get a free Six Flags ticket! It must be six hours, but not six hours straight. And it will be my first time going to Six Flags! There is just one thing that I will not, do not want to go on – the roller coasters! That is the only thing I am not going on. Are you scared to go on a roller coaster?

The Fall Festival
Ayden T.
Ms. Hall, 1st Grade

At the Fall Festival I got to do a race. I did a cannonball and a jump.

Our Snow Day
Courtney B.
Ms. Hall, 1st Grade

When we woke up we looked out our window. We saw snow everywhere! So we got up. A couple minutes later we asked our mom if we could go outside. She said yes. So we got dressed. After we got dressed our mom said we are idiots for even wanting to go outside! We got our jackets, gloves, scarves, and hats. We had two jackets. Then we went outside. First we went on the mountain in our backyard. It was hard and slippery. Then we walked around. We found ice hanging from the back of cars.

The Snow Day
Casey B.
Ms. Hall, 1st Grade

When it snowed we asked our mom if we could go outside and play in the snow. She said, "Yes, but you will freeze to death!" We had to change clothes because we were in some of our new clothes, so we changed. And then we went to play in the snow. We played freeze tag. We have big hills in our backyard. They were frozen and we tried to climb them.

Gas Station
Savannah F.
Ms. Vowell, 1st Grade

I went to the gas station. It was fun. It was cold. It rained but we stayed dry. I went with my dad. I got popcorn. It was yummy. I drank milk. I had the best time ever.

What I Like to Do
Bayli C.
Ms. Richter, 1st Grade

I like to play with my Barbies. I also like to jump on the trampoline. I like to play with my sister. I like to climb. I like to play house. I like to play my DS. I like to swing.

When I Moved Into My House
Callie A.
Ms. Richter, 1st Grade

When I moved to my house I was just born. I got lots of presents. I liked to play with my toys. I grew up in the house. When I moved in my house I was so little. When I moved in on August 18, 2003. We had a party. We had cake. I got more presents.

Me and My Friend on the Bus
Kaylee M.
Ms. Richter, 1st Grade

Me and my friend ride the bus together every day. My friend's name is Haly H. Me and Haly tell stuff to each other all the time. Me and Haly sit at the back of the bus. On the bus me and Haly take off our jackets because it is so hot. Haly makes funny jokes about stuff. One time Haly accidentally put her finger on another girl's tongue and we laughed so hard.

Swimming
Makayla A.
Ms. Richter, 1st Grade

Once when I was two I swam. I wore a vest. The water was cold at first. But the water got warm. My daddy got in too. My mommy took pictures.

My Ice Cream Day
Ryan B.
Ms. Richter, 1st Grade

I like ice cream. I like chocolate ice cream and strawberry. My best ice cream is sundae special. I love it.

What I Like to Eat
Chandler F.
Ms. Richter, 1st Grade

My favorite kind of food is pasta. I love the sauce on it. The different kinds of pasta is spaghetti and ravioli. I love it so much. When I know that's what we are eating I go crazy.

My Day Off
Legend D.
Ms. Richter, 1st Grade

On my day off I played with my sister. We played my video game. Then I went downstairs and watched TV. Next I laid down on the couch. Then I played some more with my sister. Last I went to bed.

Snow Day
Garret G.
Ms. Richter, 1st Grade

My best snow day was on Friday. I played in it. It was fun with my big brother. We had a snowball fight. I won it. We built an igloo. We got in it. We built a snowman. We built a wall.

Football Game
Matthew S.
Ms. Richter, 1st Grade

At the Falcons game one play was played twice. We got five touchdowns and we cheered. When it was halftime we stayed and watched the Dogs play. The last minute of the game the Falcons won. It was thirty to three.

Schoolwork
Brooke B.
Ms. Richter, 1st Grade

I like school because my teacher is nice to me. She is the best teacher of all. She is also pretty too. I like homework too. She gives us center time. I like my principals too. I like school. It is fun to be at school.

If I Had A Pet
Emma P.
Ms. J. O'Quinn, 2nd Grade

If I had a pet dinosaur I would name him happy. I would play with him on Fridays, Saturday, and Sunday. I would feed him fish, snacks, and shrimp. I would let him sleep in my bed with me. Happy is my baby dinosaur. He will always be my friend. He will love me. He would go to school with me. He could be a jungle gym for us.

Scary House
Ally H.
Ms. J. O'Quinn, 2nd Grade

Josh and Ally were selling brownies. When they knocked on the door the door creaked open. There was something in the hall. It was green and gooey. They went down the hall to see what it was. It was Zack. He was pretending to be a ghost. Then they heard a noise behind them. It was a real ghost. They ran to the door and the door shut. They never went to that house again.

THE END.

Ben the Ghost
Cady L.
Ms. J. O'Quinn, 2nd Grade

Once upon a time there was a ghost who was afraid of
everything. His name is Ben, but people call him Scary Cat.
One night Scary Cat saw a skeleton and the skeleton said
"Boo!" and Scary Cat said "Ahhh!" the skeleton said he
was just practicing for tomorrow because it was going to be
Halloween. Scary Cat looked in the mirror and he said "Boo!"
and he scared himself. Scary Cat decided he was going to build
a haunted house. So no said a monster to be in it. It was Ben's
turn to scare someone and he did. Ben was happy again and
lived happy ever after in Jupiter.

The Battle for the Allspark
Logan D.
Ms. J. O'Quinn, 2nd Grade

Once upon a time in a galaxy far, far away lived the
Decepticons and our heroes the Autobots. When the Autobots
crash landed in Mongolia they met Sam Whitwikey who helped
them. The Autobots came to the Earth for the Allspark cube.
There was Optimus Prime, the leader of the Autobots, and there
was Megatron, the leader of the Decepticons. The Allspark
is in a big cave in China. Sam Whitwikey bought an Autobot
named Bumblebee. Optimus Prime knew where it was, but the
Deceptacons got to it first. Then when the Autobots arrived
with Sam Whitwikey, Megatron dropped the Allspark cube.
Sam made the Allspark destroy the Deceptacons. The Autobots
won for now.

If I Were an Eskimo
Logan M.
Ms. J. O'Quinn, 2nd Grade

If I were an Eskimo living in Antarctica I would build an
igloo. I would eat frozen fish. I would make a fire for my food
and to warm up. For a weapon I would make a bow and arrow.
I would wear fur a lot.

Halloween Land
Erin B.
Ms. J. O'Quinn, 2nd Grade

If I found a land that didn't get discovered I would name it Halloween Land. There would be a witch school. There would be skeleton for a cab driver. There would be skeleton dogs. There are magic brooms for the witches. The trees would go boooo! There are goblins, mummies, and monsters.

Frosty
Shevonte J.
Ms. J. O'Quinn, 2nd Grade

Once upon a time there were 7 kids who made a snowman they named Frosty. The snowman they put a magical hat on him. Frosty came alive for the kids. They were shocked. Frosty only ate snow and all of a sudden he was talking. They were so shocked one fell on the ground.

Then Frosty said "Can I have a carrot?" They said yes, and he said some rocks too. And they said yes. One kid sneaked the snowman in the house. And they made Frosty go to sleep. The next morning he wasn't there. Frosty was playing hide-and-seek. They looked outside. He wasn't there, but Frosty was missing. All of a sudden Frosty popped out from under the shed and they found him and they lived happily ever after.

Africa
McKenzie S.
Ms. J. O'Quinn, 2nd Grade

One day I went to Africa where we found... a kangaroo with stripes. He was the prettiest thing. I named him Stripey. He was just a very small baby. We would play all day. I would pack my bag and get some food. I would bring him home and play. I would have to bring him home one day. Then one day he came back. When he came back he was a teenager. Then he could put me in his pouch. We were best friends.
The End

If I Were Principal for a Day
Milani L.
Ms. Consolie, 2nd Grade

If I were principal for a day, lunch would be at 8:30 in the morning, all the way till there's only two minutes left of school. When the students leave, the teacher would have to do the chicken dance. It goes like this: I don't want to be a chicken, I don't want to be a duck, so shake it down. Then, they would watch this movie called G-Force. Then they would leave! I would leave candy in their desk and put leprchaun foot prints on the floor. They never have homework, but the teachers do. The teachers could get sent to the principal's office. The kids can stand on the teacher's desk. Everybody gets a rock coupon at the end of the day. When the kids only have two more minutes of school, they can do whatever they want. They also can have food fights in the lunchroom. The teachers can get fired if they stop the fun. So, they put them in a room called detention while all the kids have fun. They could even throw a party and leave the mess for the teachers. That's what I would do.

The Dragon
Zoe C.
Ms. Consolie, 2nd Grade

Once upon a time, there was a crack in the sidewalk. Sitting there was an egg, not an ordinary egg, but a dragon egg. It's name was Erogon. It was growing bigger, bigger, and bigger. Soon, it was an adult dragon, and it took me around the world. Me and Erogon could talk. There were dragons everywhere we went and then I went to sleep.

The Voyage
Brianna T.
Ms. Consolie, 2nd Grade

Once upon a time, there was a woman that went on a voyage. First, she went to get one of her horses from her barn house. The horse she got out of the barn was pretty. It was a black stallion. Its whole body was covered in black. That horse was the lady's favorite horse she had ever had. The lady got on the horse and she began her voyage.

On the way to her voyage, she met people and children. She met animals like sheep, cows, bulls, and other horses. By the time she let her horse rest, she had fallen asleep. When she woke up, and the horse was carrying the woman. The horse and the woman found a hotel. They stayed for a few days. Then, they went on the voyage again and traveled. But by this time, they saw a poisonous snake. The horse ran, but the woman fell off the horse. The horse went and got the woman and they ran and ran out somewhere. They went somewhere you cannot find them. The end.

When My Nephew was Born
Makayla R.
Ms. Consolie, 2nd Grade

When my nephew was born he weighed ten pounds. His name was Kaden. Kaden was big and cute. Kaden was born October 5, 2009. Kaden was chubby.

My sister Julia had the baby. Julia is 22 years old. Julia is really pretty. Kaden is still a baby. He had black hair but then the hospital people shaved his hair so now he is growing blonde hair.

When Julia bought him a mirror he looked at it and smiled. He was so happy. Kaden is mostly always happy. Kaden weighs 15 pounds. Sometimes my mom would see Kaden. Kaden is still in the hospital. One time Santa visited Kaden. He gave Kaden a big bag of baby stuff. Kaden is coming out of the hospital this week. I am so happy that Kaden is coming home this week. I've been wondering how my sister is going to hold Kaden because he weighs 15 pounds. Kaden has chubby cheeks. Kaden screams loud. The end!

The Vacation
Logan S.
Ms. Consolie, 2nd Grade

Once upon a time there was a girl going to Florida and her name was Elizabeth. She was so excited because she knew she was going to have fun. She was five hours away from home. They were staying in a hotel and it had a pool. She had a long way to go. They finally got there and she said to her mother, "Where is our room?"

"It is 217. It is on the 2nd level."

So they got into the elevator. They got into their room, got unpacked, then they went and changed. They got into their bathing suits and went into the pool. They splashed and had fun but Elizabeth was not happy. She asked a question. It was, "Why did we come here in a hotel?"

"Well," said her mother, "because we wanted a vacation."

"Oh," said Elizabeth. "That's it? Just to have a vacation?"

"No honey. That is not all. We wanted to have fun too," mom said. "We drove for 5 hours!"

Her mother said to come out of the pool. They went to bed and had a great trip.

Lost Toe
Elyssa J.
Ms. Consolie, 2nd Grade

A long time ago there was a man who lost his toe and a girl picked it up. She knew that it was a real toe. Then she put it in her pocket and went home. When she went to bed she heard a sound and the man said, "I want my toe," but she said that it was hers. He said it again. She said to go home. When she woke up the toe was gone. Where was the toe? The girl's parents found it on her floor and came in there and asked her, "Where did you get this?" She said I found it outside yesterday.

What We Found
Austin S.
Ms. Consolie, 2nd Grade

One day Brice and I were walking down the street and we saw a crack. Inside the crack were gold dinosaur elves. We got all the gold dinosaur elves. Him and me were rich. We kept on growing and growing until we saw Big Foot and we were scared and ran away. The next day we went back down and there was nothing then we went farther and saw a car. We went in and ate barbeque. It was good. We had the best time ever. We jumped on jumps and went back home and the dinosaurs started to talk. We walked home. It was all done. The next day it happened again.

My Talking Dog
Barkim S.
Ms. Consolie, 2nd Grade

One day I had three sandwiches and then I went to get the phone. I heard something. I saw a talking dog and I was scared. So I went to call the cops but then I saw no name tags. He did not have any name or any owner. So I gave him a name tag. I gave him a name. His name is Freddy. I gave him an owner. It's me and I made him a dog house.

The Leprechaun
Johnny M.
Ms. Consolie, 2nd Grade

One day I was walking around the neighborhood and I saw a crack and a leprechaun popped out and said, "Do you want me to do your homework for you?" Then I said, "Yes." So we walked inside and we did my homework. Me and my leprechaun played a long time. We had fun together and my mom called us in to go to sleep so we came inside and we went to sleep. This morning we got up to go to school. I packed my leprechaun and we got onto the bus and walked inside the school and me and my leprechaun walked to my class.

The Leprechaun Did My Homework
Matthew L.
Ms. Consolie, 2nd Grade

One day while I was playing in the woods next to my house I met a leprechaun. I took him home and gave him something to eat. The leprechaun promised to do my homework.

I had math, science, and English to do. He worked hard on all of them and when he was finished I gave him some more food and he threw up on me.

The Robber
Payton S.
Ms. Lawrence, 2nd Grade

Last night, I awoke to a bright beam of light coming in my window. I looked outside my window. I thought it was my mom coming home from surgery. It wasn't. It was a robber. I woke up my grandmother. I told her and she screamed, "aaaaaaaaaaa," and then fainted. The robber broke into our home. We hid and the robber found us. She said, "Give me all of your money!" Then we realized it was my sister, Michelle.

My Birthday
Josh C.
Ms. Kirbow, 2nd Grade

For my birthday I went to Fun Bowl. Then we went in my house and played and swam in the pool. Then my friends left and I was sad.

My Adventures as a Sphere
Evan G.
Ms. Evans, 3rd Grade

The first time I remember leaving the place I was created was when I was taken to Dick's Sporting Goods. I was one of their most popular products. All the kids wanted me! I was a baseball. I was the best seller in the store and made the most amount of money. However, basketballs made a whole bunch of money too, better than soccer balls. I did not want to be hit to measures of waves, so I hid on the back of the shelf! My cousin, the golf ball lived very low on the bottom shelf. During summer he got bought, but after a couple of hours he was returned. You would not believe what happened to him. Someone hit him with a big metal stick, and he was black and blue with bruises. I remember one day early in the morning someone reached out and cleaned him up. Lucky for him, his adventure outside of Dick's was very short. As the sun went down, I was still here hiding on the back of the shelf.

The next morning as the sun came up, I tried to slide further back on the shelf, but there was nowhere I could go. It was a Saturday morning, one of the busiest shopping days and I had nowhere to hide. Yikes! As kids came in, they picked me up, tossed me around, got grimy stuff all over me, and put me back down. Whew! I had made it another day, or so I thought.

Just as the sun was going down and the store was about to close, another family came in. I watched as a very quiet little boy walked to where I was on the shelf. He picked me up, wiped the grime off of me, and just held me and looked at me. He took such tender care of me I thought, "Maybe going home with him would not be so bad."

My Toy
Alex C.
Ms. Ryan, 3rd Grade

One day I was looking for my toy and I noticed it was gone. Then I saw my toy on the road- crashed and smashed. I felt like I was going to kill my brother Jacob. I smashed him like he did to my toy. Now he is going to buy me a new one.

Ghost
Alexandria W.
Ms. Ryan, 3rd Grade

Once upon a time there was a girl and a boy who saw a haunted house. The boy was very freaked out because they went into the haunted house where there were ghosts. There was a board game. It had dice. They had to read it. First it said play this game carefully. If you lose the game, something bad might happen. You might be locked in a room forever.

They saw some people. They look like us.

The girl said,"Hello, my name is Emily."

The boy said, "My name is Josh."

"I am going to find you a hiding place."

"Why are we hiding?"

"I'll tell you later because the ghosts are after us."

"Why are they after us?"

"Because it thinks you lost the board game but you played it wrong"

"He's after you."

"Please tell me this isn't happening."

Dear Substitute
Shon B.
Ms. Evans, 3rd Grade

My teacher has left our schedule on her desk, but I'm going to tell you our schedule anyway. First, we do morning work. We come in quietly and get started right away. Next, we go to our specials at 8:25. When we come back, we have five minutes to eat snack. We go to the restroom, and then we do Writer's Workshop. After Writer's Workshop, we begin math. We are learning about measurement. At 11:23, we go to lunch. We are there for 30 minutes. Following lunch, we go to recess. We go outside if it is 40 degrees Fahrenheit or more, but if it is not 40 degrees or more, we do indoor recess. After recess, we do Reader's Workshop. Then after that, we do Social Studies. We are learning about a man named Thurgood Marshall. He was the first African American to work in the Supreme Court. Finally, everybody packs up and gets on the bus, car riders, or after school. I ride the bus. I hope this will help you!

Sincerely, Shon

Ahhhhhhh!
Hunter C.
Ms. Evans, 3rd Grade

It was a cold and dark afternoon. As I sat and listened to the rain hit the roof, I was glad that school was almost over! The bell just went off! But wait! It was the emergency lockdown bell.

"Ahhhhh!" I screamed. Everyone screamed!

Then the teacher said, "Quiet!" Then a silent shadow came by the door. "Get back away from the door!" Then after that another shadow came by the door. Everyone was as scared as can be. I wasn't, but I just played along.

"Stay calm children," the teacher said. But then the bell stopped ringing. Then the power went out. I looked for the yellow bag. Then I found it. There was a flashlight and a first aid kit, but then the intercom came on.

"Don't worry students. It's just a drill." Then we all breathed a sigh of relief.

The Scared Kitten
Madison S.
Ms. Evans, 3rd Grade

The scared kitten was meowing loudly. A large dog was running toward her. She shook with fear, but was too weak to move. She tried crawling weakly across the floor, her tongue hanging out of her mouth. She was almost to safety, only one more step to go, and she fell down. The kitten had crawled safely under the table. Underneath was her cozy bed made of carpet with her food and milk next to it.

"Sip, sip," she drank her milk and then she heard footsteps coming closer and closer. Then the door opened. It was her owners, Jane, Joe, Mrs. Lane, and Mr. Lane. There was a cage in Mr. Lanes hand. "Oh no! Another dog," she thought. It was playing with a bell. It was a girl dog. She was very special. She had a collar that said "America" on it, and she was a blue dog with red, white, and blue spots! Jane let it out of the cage.

Joe said, "Welcome to your new home!" Oh no! It was another dog! The puppy got out and played with the other dog. They both ran quickly toward her, poor kitten. She quickly drank her milk and ate her food. She knew it was back to her hiding spot! She feared she would have to get used to her new spot!

The Scary Morning
Zachary C.
Ms. Scarbrough, 3rd Grade

One morning I heard a crash. I ran to my backyard to look. It was a space ship. It took me to planet X. I saw aliens. They locked me up so I planned an escape. I snuck past the guards and got in the spaceship. It was set for Mars. It flew. There were many more aliens but this time it wasn't a couple of aliens, it was thousands. It was war. By night they were all gone. I stayed on their planet. In the morning it took me to Neptune. There were no aliens. I spend a couple of days there. I found a tiny bug. He told me some beasts were going to attack me so he gave me something tiny and round. It flew. It took me to Pluto. There I threw the thing on the ground. It turned into a huge beast. It fought the other beasts. I got back in the spaceship. It flew me home. I was so glad to be back with my mom, dad, sister, and my puppy.

The Best Day
Anais C.
Ms. Scarbrough, 3rd Grade

My best day was when we drew on our desk and the other fun thing was Grandparents Day. I love Grandparents Day because you get to meet everybody's grandparents. The other fun thing was school. I love it and school is fun. My grandparents couldn't come because they live in St. Thomas. I am going to St. Thomas next summer.

Scary Night
Jeremy S.
Ms. Scarbrough, 3rd Grade

It was a scary night. The wolves were howling. Me and my friend flew in a haunted mansion. There were bats and monsters. There were good monsters and bad monsters. The bad, bad, bad monster was the baddest of all of them. There was a good monster and he was the best of all. So I went upstairs and opened a door and there were a lot of vampires. I was so scared and my friend was not behind me. So I went downstairs and he was not there. I looked everywhere then I found a cave in the way. There were two hallways. I went down one then I went down the other. There he was. He was looking for me too. The the bad monster came. He went right past us. I went back upstairs and opened another door and there were a lot of hungry wolves.

The New Blond Girl
Bria B.
Ms. Scarbrough, 3rd Grade

A little blond girl looked scared at her new school. Her name is Morgan and my name is Bria. Morgan is really nice, smart, and loves to read books like me. Morgan is from Virginia but now she lives in Georgia. We are neighbors and we are in the same class.

Morgan is a funny girl and she also loves to climb trees. She has a sister who is six years old and Morgan is eight years old. She also has two one year old twin brothers. Morgan is the oldest. She has eight puppies, five kittens, and a two year old pony. She loves to eat sweets. If Morgan's mommy doesn't make sweets every once in a while Morgan will get real, real mad. Also, every day Morgan comes outside because she does her homework at school or on the bus.

Morgan's dad is at his job and Morgan is at my house having a sleepover. She brought her puppies and kittens. We played and played until finally we went to sleep. In the morning we heard barking, purring, and felt licking. Morgan's dad was there to pick us up. So we hurried to put on our clothes and eat. Then we went to Morgan's house. Morgan and I swam in the pool while her dad watched us. It was real fun. Morgan doesn't have any friends except for me.

The Old, Abandoned House
Madison R.
Ms. Scarbrough, 3rd Grade

It was a dark, spooky Wednesday night. There was a storm up ahead. I was on my way home until I heard a loud CRASH! It came from the old, abandoned house.

It had never made such a sound before. There had always been creaks and soft booms. I headed toward the house.

A few minutes later I stepped inside and realized that it was…some old furniture that had fallen. There was dust and cobwebs on the chairs. Also there were spiders on the couches and TV.

After I left, I heard it again. I decided to look at it the next day. The next morning the police and I went back to the house.

When we got there there were some robbers leaving. We quickly tried to catch them but they were too fast.

Later that day we went back. There were the robbers again! This time we caught them. We got them to confess. They spit out the whole story.

The chief took them to jail and gave me an official jr. police badge. That's the story of the old, old abandoned house and me.

The Noise I Heard
Colby F.
Ms. Scarbrough, 3rd Grade

One morning I heard a loud noise. It was so loud it woke me up then I went downstairs to see what the sound was. When I got downstairs the noise was off then it came back on. It kept coming on and off and on and off and on and off and then it stopped. Then it came back on. I looked everywhere except in my brother's room. Next I went upstairs and went into my brother's room and the sound was my brother screaming.

Yard Work
April H.
Ms. Scarbrough, 3rd Grade

One day I went outside. Then I raked leaves. Then I put the leaves in a garbage bag. Then I put the house garbage outside by the leaves. Then the garbage man took away the garbage.

What Did I Hear?
Abigail J.
Ms. Scarbrough, 3rd Grade

One morning I heard a sound. I did not know what it was. I looked all around the house to see if anything fell. I did not see anything that fell.

My mom said, "Time for school."

I said, "Ok," then the bus came.

When I got on the bus I sat with my friend Lexy. We started talking about how much we love tater tots but I totally forgot about the sound. Lexy and I were also talking about if she could come over later. I said, "Sure!"

I had a great day but when me and Lexy got to my house I heard the sound. She said, "What is that sound?"

I said, "Well, I don't know."

She said, "Let's find out." So we went on a hunt about the sound.

I said, "Now we only have to look in the bathroom," after we went on a hunt for the sound everywhere else in the house. We saw in the bathroom the water running.

She said, "That must be the sound."

I said, "It probably is." The two of us were the best friends and now we are the bestest friends!

The Robot
Nakyah G.
Ms. Scarbrough, 3rd Grade

One morning I heard a cracking sound. I went outside to see what it was but when I got outside it was too late. I saw a cracking robot chicken that can jump high in the sky. Then I went inside the house.

My room was a mess because the robot jumped on my new, clean, made-up bed. He also took my toys out of my toybox and put them on the floor. Then I had to pick all my toys up and put them back in the toybox. Now I am making up my bed.

"You are going back where you came from or belong."

"Why?" said the robot.

"Because you messed up my room."

"I am so sorry."

"Oh! It's o.k." I said. "Let's go. Good-bye."

The Best Day
Dallas S.
Ms. Scarbrough, 3rd Grade

What was the best day you ever had? The best day I ever had is my pool party! I had a blast there. I had a lot of my friends there and a lot of stuff to play with. And I had a lot of decorations there and some toys to play with in the pool and a water bottle fight. It is just like a water gun fight, but you just poke a hole in the middle with a pen and squeeze the water bottle at someone and make a water gun! I had a lot of presents and a big cake. The time it was nighttime. We all had the party at my house. When we were leaving we saw five deer. They are a family of deer. When we went to my house we were having a party so all of us went home.

Dog Catching
Joshua K.
Ms. Murdock, 3rd Grade

Dog catching is a really good sport for dogs. Dog catching helps dogs get healthy and more active. Dogs can jump high and catch a Frisbee and have lots of fun and can see and hear really well.

People throw the Frisbee. Dogs can't throw the Frisbee and in order to catch the Frisbee the dog has to go wherever the Frisbee goes to catch it. They also have to jump in a clean space so they don't bump or hit anything or someone. They also have to have sharp teeth so they can bite the Frisbee. And they need to be strong and their legs need to be strong.

A Horse Who Got Changed into a Human
Sara S.
Ms. Murdock, 3rd Grade

One day there was a horse named Leila. One day she was walking to the bridge. She saw something at the bridge. When she got there it was a witch. The witch changed her into a human.

One morning she woke up. She said, "Where am I?" Leila looked at herself. She yelled and said, "My tail and hooves are gone!"

The witch told her that it changed her into a human. Leila ran away and changed back into a horse and then she lived happily ever after.

I Had a Dream
Jeffrey O.
Ms. Murdock, 3rd Grade

"Is it bedtime?" said Max.

"Yep." said Max's mom.

"OK. Good night," said Max. Max went into his bed. He fell right to sleep. Max suddenly had a dream that he was in a place called CandyLand. There was all the candy in the world, but there was this licorice man who did not like candy! Max did not care! But the licorice man was planning to steal all the candy, but Max was quick. Max had a plan to save CandyLand. He built soldiers out of candy and vehicles. It worked. Max saved CandyLand. He got a little bit of candy and left.

Max woke up. He told his mom and dad about his dream in the morning.

Blue Moon
Michaela M.
Ms. Murdock, 3rd Grade

Blue Moon was a blue goldfish. He had always been teased by all of the other goldfish, but the goldfish that teased Blue Moon the most were Goldie, Goldman, and Jeffy. Blue Moon was teased about his color, his name, and his personality. Goldie was a girl that was conceited and she was mean to every fish in the whole, wide sea! Goldman just has the whole collection of Nemo Chronicles. Jeffy is in the special fish school classes. Blue Moon has a beautiful blue color. Blue Moon tried to put on gold fish coloring. That backfired because he turned gray. He tried to put on a goldfish costume but that didn't work because the costume was too small for him and it tore apart. Blue Moon just gave up.

Then all of the fish in the sea got caught by a net! It was all up to Blue Moon! He went under the sun's reflection in the water and he made a laser. The laser shot open the bag and all the fish came rushing out. The fish swam up to Blue Moon and Hip, Hip, Hoorayed him and Blue Moon was never teased again and had lots and lots of friends!

The Time I Went to Ms. Frank's House
Alexis K.
Ms. Murdock, 3rd Grade

I went to Ms. Frank's house to ride horses. I rode Honey. She is sweet just like real honey. She was trained so she was good with me on her back. After that Katie and me made pizza. We put a lot of stuff on it. Then Ms. Frank put the pizza in the oven, so Katie and I went upstairs. We went in her playroom. We played Wii Sing It. It was so fun! Then we had our pizza and hot cocoa. It was so good. Then we went to see Pepper, their pig. Pepper nibbles, so watch out! Then we went upstairs and played hangman. The word was Ms. Frank. Lucas came back from hunting with Derek, Ms. Frank's son. Then we had to go.

Lucy Saves the Day
Mary G.
Ms. Murdock, 3rd Grade

This is a story about Lucy. She is different from other horses because she only has three legs. Since Lucy is different nobody wanted her around. So Lucy walked away. For the first couple of days they were happy Lucy had gone. That night Lucy came out from her hiding place for some food. She made sure that she didn't wake up anyone. When she was done she went back to her hiding place for some sleep. When everyone woke up they saw some foot prints in the dirt. They looked like wolf prints. So when it was night the other horses sent some horses to look for strange things. Now Lucy could not come out from her hiding place. Then Lucy heard a strange noise from the bushes. The guard horses were looking the other way. She saw a head pop out from the bushes. Right then she knew it was a wolf. She ran from her hiding place to tell everyone about the wolf. Everyone was scared to hear about the wolf. Then Lucy turned around and ran to the wolf. When she got there she jumped up and down. The wolf ran away and everyone was happy to have Lucy back.

Goldilocks and the Three Bears
Chris M.
Ms. Ryan, 3rd Grade

Once upon a time there were three bears. There was a mommy bear, a daddy bear, and a baby bear. One day the daddy bear made some porridge. It was hot so mommy bear, daddy bear, and baby bear went for a walk while it cooled off.

Then a little girl named Goldielocks was walking in the woods. She was the house and snuck in. She ate all the porridge then tried sitting in daddy bear's chair, then mommy bear's chair, and then baby bear's chair. When she sat in baby bear's chair it fell apart.

Next she tried their beds. First she tried daddy bear's bed, and she didn't like it. Then she tried mommy bear's bed, and she liked hers a little bit. Then she tried baby bear's bed and she loved it. Then she fell asleep.

When the three bears got home they saw her in baby bear's bed. Then she woke up and ran off. The end.

Sports
Hayli B.
Ms. Ryan, 3rd Grade

I like sports as much as everyone else does. I love to play soccer! I haven't signed up yet, but I might sign up this month. My mom says I have to play softball because my mom played, and her mom played, plus my cousin, Autumn, played also. So it's like a cycle. I like soccer a little more than softball.

My Dad, Paul, played football and baseball. He played baseball for about three years. He played football from middle school to his first year of college. He had a lot of fun. He's thirty-one, now. He sometimes plays for fun. One time he tried to teach me to throw the balls but I was only about four or five! He tried his best!

My pa-paw is into golf. I kind of like it, it's interesting. So does my Na-Naw. I've been playing for almost 3 years. The only golfer I know about is Tiger Woods, and I knew zilch about him!

I'm going to be the second person in my family to play soccer because my cousin Chase is already playing. Now my sister wants to sign up, which is pretty good.

If you like soccer, good for you. If you want to sign up, ask your parents. I heard that there are going to be soccer sign ups sometime this week.

The Five Little Fish and the Big Bad Monster
Bryce, G.
Ms. Ryan, 3rd Grade

Once there were five fish. Their mom was tired of them living there so she told them to go get girlfriends. There was a fight and one of the fish put tape on his mother's mouth and left.

A monster came in and ate her. He spit her clothes out and the tape.

The monster came to the first fish and the monster busted down the door. The fish swam out, and threw his girlfriend at the monster. The monster ate her.

The first fish ran in the house and the four fish were looking at him. Then the shark busted opened the door and the fish went flying to the second fish. The three fish beat up the shark.

Dirtbikes
Rylan S.
Ms. Ryan, 3rd Grade

I race dirtbikes on my track. You have to do five laps. Sometimes I got beat by a girl but now I am beating her in dirtbike racing. Now I get paid for getting the hole shot or winning. Plus my next race is not until February 6, 2010. There are a lot of different colors- red, black, yellow, orange, blue, and green. Dirtbikes go from 45, 75, 105, 125, 145, and it keeps going on to 450's.

Snow Day
Jackson L.
Ms. Hurndon, 3rd Grade

One day my brother, my sister, and I went sledding. First, we got our jackets, hoods, snow boots, gloves, and scarves. Next, we went to the backyard to sled because our backyard has a lot of hills. Plus, the backyard had a lot of snow! We sled down about 20 times. We also did a few wipeouts. After mom and dad got back from shopping, we had to come in to get warm and eat lunch. Later that day, we went back outside and had more fun!

The Dream
Jourdan C.
Ms. Hurndon, 3rd Grade

One dark night, a boy named Jake was playing outside with his friends Nate, Lakin, and Nahja. They are all 14 years old. They were playing football. Jake and Nate were on one team and Nahja and Lakin were on the other team. Jake and Nahja were the fastest so they got to be team captains. The game was being played at the Georgia Dome. They got to play at the Dome because one of their other friend Jourdan's dad was the manager of the Atlanta Falcons. Jourdan was always the all time quarter back. That is because he has a very good arm. He can throw from mid-field to the in zone. In the first play of the game, Nahja and Lakin got the ball on the 20 yard line and the very next play was an interception by Jake.

Jourdan's dad had to run home quickly. Their neighborhood was just across the street from the Dome. Jourdan's dad gave him the keys so they had access to everything in the Dome! Jourdan and his friends had an idea to get something to drink then go to the locker room after the game. After they were done with all that then they were going to listen to the Black Eyed Peas over the loud speaker. At half time, Jake's team was losing 14 to 7. In the third quarter, the game was tied with four minutes left. In the end Nahja's team won 35 to 28. Then they did what they said they would do. Nate woke up really fast and realized that it was all a dream.

Crispy the Dragon
Joshua A.
Ms. Hurndon, 3rd Grade

There once was a dragon named Crispy. He was black and blue with a white head. His legs were green and he flew around blowing fire on everything. He was sixty feet tall with very long and wide wings. Crispy was an angry and sad dragon. He was very lonely. He couldn't make friends because he burned everything down. He burned the crops, cars, trees, houses, and even people! No one knew what Crispy would burn next. People were scared of Crispy. They would run and hide when he flew nearby. Crispy then started to think about what he was doing. He realized that burning things wasn't a way to make friends. So he started helping people by giving them rides and not blowing fire on them. He even protected them from other dragons. Crispy then made friends with people in the town.

Peaches
CJ C.
Ms. Hurndon, 3rd Grade

Peaches is a Jack Russell Terrier. She is not an ordinary dog. She is a super dog. Peaches can do many special things. She saves lives. Peaches can fly. She can fly faster than a thunder bolt. She can fly higher than the clouds. She can even fly down through the Earth and outer space. Peaches can also run fast. She can run through monsters. She makes them dizzy. Peaches has a killer touch. She uses the wosie hold on the bad guys. This paralyzes them. She uses the smoshy finger to kill her enemies. They die in one second. If I was you, I wouldn't mess with Peaches.

Stray
Elizabeth M.
Ms. Hurndon, 3rd Grade

Hi, my name is Prince. My mom named me that because I am royalty. I am also a stray, living the life and loving every minute of it! Wait, I got that scent, scent of the slammer. I gotta get out of here and run fast so I don't get caught. Hey, I smell meat. Follow the scent to get the meat. As I grab it BOOM! A net slammed right in front of me. Oh great, what's that the 5th or 6th time this year to have to go to jail. I really got to get a life. As they put me in the truck, I hear something next to me crying. It must be another dog. I looked through the holes and see a Chihuahua. "What's your name little guy?" I asked. I regret to say I heard a squeaky voice say, "Minnie." I thought to myself that suits her. When we get to the shelter we wait forever and finally we get in our kennel. We sleep and then a new day!

As I wake up, I smell food. I look and there is some food. Yum, Yum! I have got to think of a way to get out of here. I have been here before so I know what to do. When these guys take you on a leash they do not have a good grip on it. Here they come to give me a break from this kennel. As I exit out, I run and pull hard. I am FREE. Oh great, I hear something.

What is that sound? I look back and see Minnie! I stop so she will quit barking. Minnie says, "I am coming with you!" I told her "I guess I can make room for one more on all my adventures. We had a great day being free. I found a spot to pee and as I was BOOM! Oh great, a net! Looks like the slammer again for me.

The Haunted Mansion
Ashley G.
Ms. Hurndon, 3rd Grade

Once there was a girl named Ashley. One day Ashley and her friends, Abby, Allison, and Aliva were walking home from the ice cream shop. They took a short cut through the woods. They thought it would take them home but it didn't. It took them to a creepy, old mansion. Abby told her friends that she had read about this old place. She told them that a boy went in there and never came out but her friends didn't seem to listen. They walked up to the door about to ring the door bell when the door opened very quickly. They all screamed! "We should go back," Allison said. But the girls were too scared to even move. Each girl was terrified. Aliva walk in there when her even though her friends told her not to. When they were all inside the house the door closed by itself. This made them even more scared.

"Wwwhhhhooooooooiiiiiiissstttthhhheeeerrrree?" asked a strange voice. They all froze and then looked up to the top of the stairs and saw a ghost.

The ghost then said, "You have entered a mansion full of ghosts. You must leave or else..." The girls turned around to run to go out the door but it was too late. The ghost had locked the door.

Allison whispered, "We should hide." They all agreed so they ran to a coat closet. They didn't know if they were about to die or not. After waiting for a few minutes, Aliva cracked the door open. Then they realized that a ghost was in the closet with them.

"Go home nooooowww!" the ghost said. Abby ran out of the closet and towards the door. The door was unlocked now. Her friends followed her.

As they were running in the yard they noticed that they all had gravestones just sitting in the ground. "How did these get here?" Abby asked.

Ashley replied, "I don't know but it is very creepy."
"Who cares! Run for it!" yelled Aliva. They ran really fast
back through the woods and back to their homes. All of the
girls tried to tell their parents but their parents all said it was
not true and to quit telling jokes.

A couple of days later the girls decided to go back to the
creepy mansion but it was gone. They started to walk towards
where the mansion was and ran into something. They then
realized that the mansion was there it was just invisible. They
searched around to find the door and then went inside. This
time the ghost kicked the girls out. The girls went back home
and made a plan.

A few weeks later they returned back to the house and
blew it up. Everyone had nothing to worry about anymore.
They all had a wonderful life after that terrifying time. Aliva
made the soccer team, Allison became president of the school,
Abby got in the science club, and Ashley became a professional
gymnast. The girls remained friends forever.

Snakezilla
Devian M.
Ms. Hurndon, 3rd Grade

One day in New York, 2023, two scientists were working
on something to make creatures heal faster. They thought they
had the right potion this time but when they tested it on a king
cobra all it did was make the king cobra grow arms, legs, and
get bigger. Dr. Ock ran for help while Dr. Debenderfer stood
frozen in fear.

Project X carnivore had failed. When Dr. Ock had returned
all he saw was a hole in the wall, chemicals on the floor,
and a bloody lab coat. He called the president and told him
what happened. He explained to the president what Project X
carnivore was about and how it went wrong. He also told the
president that Snakezilla had eaten his partner and was now
running freely.

So the president sent the United States Army to either
destroy Snakezilla or contain him. Later at the lab Dr. Ock
was getting DNA samples from the hole in the wall. He found
out that Snakezilla had stepped in other chemicals like fast
grow, extra agility, and the power to spit poison. Then Dr. Ock
stepped out of the lab and walked beside the footprints and
watched them get bigger. Then he saw poison coming down out

of the sky. He also saw missiles and bullets and heard stomps that shook New York. Then he saw Snakezilla looking in his eyes.

General Scar came up behind Dr. Ock and said, "It is a beautiful sight but it must be destroyed." Then he walked away. By then Snakezilla had killed all of the soldiers and turned around and saw General Scar in a giant robot.

Dr. Ock turned to General Scar and said, "You cannot kill Snakezilla, the only thing we can do is use a potion. I had been working on it all night and I know it will work."

Dr. Ock said, "You only got one shot, if you don't kill him in your first shot we are all dead!" So General Scar dipped his knife in the cure and charged at Snakezilla but dropped the cure right in front of Snakezilla.

Snakezilla hissed, "Game over."

Right then out of the sea came other snakes that had been tested on. General Scar asked Dr. Ock, "How many did you test on?"

Dr. Ock replied, "Fifty."

Two years later, China was in flames, New York was completely destroyed, and the world was at its knees. In the end, only one person survived...Dr. Debenderfer.

Twisted Ankle
Gabriella C.
Ms. Hurndon, 3rd Grade

It all began while I was studying in first grade at home. The door was open so my sister came in my room. She took my pillow so I started to run after her. I kept chasing her until I got my pillow. I got tired so I began to walk slowly back to my room. She caught up to me! As I was reaching for my door somehow I twisted my ankle. I then hopped to the bed. When my mom came in my room to tell me it was time for bed, she asked, "What's wrong?"

I replied, "I twisted my ankle." The next day I couldn't go to school. That morning my mom put ice on my ankle. The next day we went to Henry Medical Center because it was not better. They all said that I hopped like a bunny. They gave me a long bandage. We then went to the store and found Icy Hot. The next day I went to school. We watched *Polar Express* and I was the one that got to put my feet on a pillow.

Dreaming
Miranda S.
Ms. Armstrong, 4th Grade

One day I got up to get a drink of milk but it was not milk.
It was rotten milk. I went to sleep after, or I thought I did. I
went to the kitchen to get juice. But it was icky bugs that were
frozen. I know what you are going to say, "Yuck!" I got hungry
and I went to get macaroni and cheese. It was not macaroni and
cheese. It was water and a sock! So, I figured out that I was not
asleep.

The Monster Under Her Bed!!!!
Ashlyn H.
Ms. Elmer, 4th Grade

One night, a girl named Juney had just gotten home from
her private school. She took a shower and brushed her hair and
teeth. When she was walking to her bed she heard a growling
noise. She thought it was her dog, but it wasn't. It was the
Boglely Woglely Monster!
She had never heard of the Boglely Woglely Monster, so
she laid down and tried to go to sleep. All she could hear was
"GRRRR! GRRRR! GRRRR!" over and over. Then, he came
out. She saw two glowing eyes. Juney screamed! Her parents
ran into her room in a flash but didn't see or hear anything.
They went back to their room.
She heard her dog barking and growling under her bed.
She got up. It was 1:00 in the morning. She was really tired
and had to go to school the next day. She got a flash light and
looked under her bed. The monster grabbed her and ate her.
All that was left of her was a slipper. That was the last time
anyone ever saw Juney. GRRRRRRRRRR!

The Haunted House
Austin Q.
Ms. Elmer, 4ᵗʰ Grade

One day I was walking through a scary house that I thought was haunted. Did I mention that I was alone? Anyway, I heard someone slam a door so I ran to the attic. I tried to call the police. Something or someone smashed the window.

"I guess I'll have dinner here and call some friends," I said to myself. Smash! "Or not!"

The next day I decided I was going to call the ghosts to tell them to get me out of this place! I went to the car. I had no idea that the car was haunted, too. So I got in the car. I did not start the car; it went up and flew into the air. I was screaming for help. Then there was a helicopter over me. It fell out of the sky. The car fell, too!

I went back to that house two weeks later, and this time lamps were floating in mid-air. There was one ghost that kept fooling me. Two days later, I called in ghost hunters and they set up motion sensors. For twenty-four hours straight one hundred ghosts walked past it. So, there are over one hundred ghosts in that house. I will keep going over there to see if the place is still haunted.

The End (or not?)

The Disaster Mess
Deonte J.
Ms. Elmer, 4ᵗʰ Grade

My mother told me that I had to clean my four year old sister's room. I didn't want to because my sister's room was horrible. She had a lot of pencils under her bed. She didn't want anyone to see her collection. She had a lot of clothes on the floor and in her closet. She would always sleep in my room because her room was cold. She sleeps a lot and never makes her bed. She gets a lot of attention. She is always playing in her sheets and jumping on her bed.

I cleaned up the pencils and put them in a heart shaped collection box. I fixed her room vent so it wouldn't be cold. I told her that if she didn't hang up her clothes, the Boogey man would come for her! I also made her promise not to jump on her bed so the Boogey Man wouldn't come get her. Now she doesn't get extra attention anymore. Now I really love my sister.

The Pop Tart
Grace G.
Ms. Elmer, 4th Grade

This morning, my dog woke me up. So, I got ready for
school. I went downstairs to eat breakfast and decided to have
a pop tart. I opened it up and put in the toaster. When my
pop tart came out of the toaster, lighting flashed and thunder
cracked. I screamed, "Aaagh! Evil pop tart!" I wondered why
there was only one in the pack.
    "It is the great, evil Dr. Pop Tart!" the pop tart said.
    "Mom!" Brooke yelled.
    "What Brooke?"
    "Quick come down here!"
    "What is the problem?"
    "I just made a talking pop tart."
    "A talking pop tart?" Mom asked.
    "A talking pop tart, mom." I told her.
    "I don't see a talking pop tart."
    "What? It was right here! Where'd it go?"
    Brooke found the pop tart. She put it in her back pack and
went off to school. When Brooke was on the bus, she took the
pop tart out of her back pack and stared at it for a long time.
Then, the bus monitor saw her with it and took it away. She
said, "No eating on the bus."
    "See you later! It is time for me to rule the world! Hey,
by the way, will you cook some more pop tarts of that brand
while you're at it? I won't be back!"
    I needed my pop tart back. I couldn't let it rule the world.
Just the thought of it…the pop tarts eating us instead of us
eating them. It gave me the shivers to just think about it. So I
spoke up for the world's sake! "Excuse me ma'am, can I have
my pop tart back?"
    "Yes but keep it in your back pack," the bus monitor said.
So Brooke put it in her back pack.
    "Phew! That was a close call." When Brooke got to
school, it was the same boring old day.
    Brooke decided to walk home from school that day. On
her way home she stopped by PetsMart. The store clerk
wondered how old Brooke was. "Um, how old are you
ma'am?"
    "How old are you sir!?"
    "Good point," he said. "Here's your bird cage ma'am," the
store clerk said.

"Thanks and have a great day!" Brooke yelled.

"Sure you too," the clerk said suspiciously.

When Brooke got home, she gave the pop tart medicine to make him sleepy. After he went to sleep, she put him in the bird cage in case he woke up. After she did that, she left the room. A few minutes later, she returned. Not much to her surprise, he was still sleeping. "I had a feeling he would still be sleeping after a long day trying to escape my back pack, wasting energy, and melting. He probably just wants to lay on the cold cage floor and sleep," Brooke said. She was starting to wonder why he had turned light blue after being dark red all day. Maybe it was because he calmed down.

"Okay, I got mom's surgery mask, a spoon, and a fork," Brooke said while reading her list silently to herself. (To Do List: 1. Shape head to circle with fork and spoon. 2. Find string and tie hands to perch in cage. 3. Get door knob thing and hang over head in shoulders.) She layed the pop tart (A.K.A. Dr. Pop tart) on her desk and began operating. When she was done, to her surprise, it worked! She put him in the cage, still sleeping. She got the string and doorknob thing and did exactly as she planned.

Finally, the pop tart woke up. He didn't notice his head but he did notice everything else. Meanwhile, Brooke was in the kitchen. A few minutes later her mom walked in the door. "Hi sweetie!" said Mom.

"Hi Mom! Did you get my angel food cake tasting pop tarts?" asked Brooke.

"I sure did," said Mom.

"Can I have one?" Brooke asked.

"Yes, you can" said Mom.

So Brooke got one out and put it in the toaster. When it came out, all the lights went off and there was a spotlight on the pop tart. This pop tart was yellow, wore a white gown and had a halo on its head. The pop tart started to sing "la la la la, Oh, I love to love and I love playing my harp."

"Who are you and what's up with that harp of yours?" Brooke asked.

"I don't know, but it's fun to love!" said the pop tart.

Brooke taped a piece of paper down the middle of the bird cage and put the good pop tart on one side and the evil pop tart on the other side. She checked the receipt, and it said "buy one, get one free". So she went back to the store to show the man the receipt and she got another bird cage for free.

When she got home, she reached in the first cage and got

the good pop tart and put it in the new cage and took the paper down from the bad pop tart's cage. Then, Brooke went to sleep.

That night her mom came in to check on her and she saw the pop tarts. She said to herself, "Oh my goodness! She knows she's not supposed to have food in her room! I'll just have to get rid of that right away!"

When Brooke's mom did that, she put it in the kitchen trash can which was by the toaster! So the pop tarts got out.

"So this is where it ends," said Love.

"I guess so," said Dr. Pop Tart. "Let's get toasty!" Both pop tarts started making their own brands. When it was over they each had their own army of their own pop tart brand.

Brooke heard a ruckus in the kitchen. First she thought it was her dog, but then she noticed the pop tarts were missing and the cage doors were open. "Mom!" Brooke whispered to herself. Then she went downstairs. The good pop tarts were huddled up and talking; the evil side was doing the same. "Oh brother!" said Brooke.

"What do you mean 'Oh brother'? I didn't do this!" Brooke's brother Max said.

"Where did you come from?" Brooke asked him.

"I was watching your cool pop tarts have a war."

"Go back to bed Max," Brooke said.

"No!"

"Yes!"

"No!"

"Yes!"

"No, no, no, no!!! La la la la la! I can't hear you!!!"

Finally Brooke's mom and dad came downstairs to the kitchen. "What is all this about?" Brooke's dad asked.

"Well, the other day I made a talking pop tart and-" Brooke said with her dad cutting her off at the "and."

Her dad said "And.....I think you're acting crazy. Now everybody back to bed!" Brooke's dad said.

Brooke got all the pop tarts and took them up to her room. Luckily, they both only made 4. "Some army," Brooke was thinking to herself. She put the armies in the cages. Then.... BEEP BEEP BEEP BEEP....BAM! "My alarm? I was sleeping?? Whew!" Brooke went downstairs and there was Max, sitting with all 10 talking pop tarts.

"Hi Brooke" Max and all the pop tarts said.

"AGHHHH!!" Brooke yelled...then fainted. When she woke up and her mom told her she'd screamed and fainted, there was Max…with no pop tarts. "I had a dream about having a dream?" Brooke said. "WEIRD!"

Katie
Kaleigh J.
Ms. Elmer, 4th Grade

Once upon a time, there was a girl named Katie. She was rich. She did not like money, because people were using her for her money. That's why she didn't have many friends. Katie did not know that some people did not have money, because she had been rich her whole life.

Some days Katie would sit in a corner at school because she did not have anybody to play with. Then her dad saw that she was lonely and bought her a journal. When she began to write in the journal, she looked happy. She wasn't happy. She saw her dad looking so she acted like she was happy.

Katie had a list of things she did not like. Sometimes she would cry because she was alone. She hated being alone. She hated it so much that she ran away. She got some clothes, food, and a tent. She wrote a note to her dad saying:

Dear Dad,

I cannot live this way – alone and unhappy – so I am running away.

Love, Katie

The next day her dad saw the note and read it. He started to cry. He called 911, and the police came over to start looking for Katie. They found her. She went home and moved to a smaller house and made friends. She said she was not alone anymore…

Until she was good at talking and made fun of her friends. They got mad and were not her friends. Then she was in her alone stage again. Her friends were too mad to even talk to her. She was alone and sad. She tried everything to get her friends back. She even tried to dress up as a clown, but it didn't work. Then she begged to be friends with them. They said yes. She was not sad anymore.

Shazam!
Nicolette W.
Ms. Elmer, 4th Grade

"Ahhh!" Shelly, the most popular girl in the whole school, screamed.

Her assistant, Mary, asked, "What's wrong?"

"My hair!" Shelly said.

"What about your hair?"

"It's ugly and flat," I say as I walk into the girl's restroom.

"Well, well, well, look who's talking Hannah Banana."

Yes, that's my name, Hannah. People tease me because I get all A's. Middle school, (sigh) what a strange grade to be in. People tease you for nothing.

Shelly says, "I say that you put a sock in your mouth, because it obviously has no control."

"Well, I suggest you eat an apple instead of all that meat you've been eating. That all goes to your hips." I walked out not looking back.

"What if someone finds out about the cat fight you two had?" my best friend Alley asked.

"I don't know," I said as I took a scoop of potato salad for my tray.

"Well, there's one thing I know," Alley said. "I'm not eating that goop."

I chuckled. "Don't worry," I said, still laughing. "I won't make you, so you're covered."

As she stepped out the door, SPLAT! Food splattered all over Shelly Wickmen's shirt. *Well one thing is covered*, I thought.

As Shelly, Alley, and I walked into our school principal's office, I thought that my principal would not believe me. But she's understanding. I'm sure she'll understand. So, I told her what happened, and, of course, she understood. Shelly called her mom and asked her to bring some clothes. Alley and I went back to class.

"That was close," Alley said.

"Not even," I said.

THE NEXT DAY…

"Oh my gosh!" Alley cried. "I totally forgot about the quiz!"

"What!" I yelled. "I reminded you like ten times."

"Oh well, I hope I get lucky."

"Let's all hope you do," I said.

The very next day she ran to my locker and said, "I got an A+ on my quiz!"

"What? An A+?" I said in amazement. "I got a B. I still don't know why Mr. Cooper thinks that Christopher Columbus lived in Portugal."

"Whatever, I guess I got lucky."

"Goody for you," I said. "Come on, let's get some lunch."

The next day, Alley and I went to our first day of cheerleading. We went to the field to practice. As soon as we got in a pyramid position, Alley said, "S, H, A, Z, A, M! That spells SHAZAM!" as she got toppled over by other cheerleaders. Sadly, we were the only ones that got broken bones.

As soon as we got up, doctors carried us into an ambulance. When we woke up at the hospital, we were crowded by doctors, family, and friends. I wondered how we had gotten in the hospital. As I sat up, I noticed I had a broken arm and a cast. Alley did, too. As I thought, I remembered the tragic cheerleading accident and wondered if any other girls were injured.

Of course cheerleaders gossiped about Alley. Everyone started saying shazam – except for me, of course. As we walked to our lockers, Alley said, "I'm sick of it! It's like shazam sickness!"

When I opened my locker, there, in red paint, it said "bloody murder".

"I swear it was there!"

"Okay, I believe you. I just don't know who would do such a thing."

"Me neither."

"Hey," said Alley, "let's be like Sherlock Holmes and be detectives."

"Oh, what a splendid idea," I said in the best British accent I could manage.

"Alley, I found a clue!"

"Really? What is it?"

"A note! It says, 'Meet me at the girl's locker room in the gym'."

"So she has to be a girl."

At the gym, we went into the girl's locker room and found the very last clue of our mystery…Shelly Wickmen – no wonder.

The Best Friends
Saree B.
Ms. Elmer, 4th Grade

Once upon a time, there were these two best friends.
They've been friends since kindergarten. They were older now
– nine and ten. Their names were Saree and Kaleigh. Kaleigh
was ten; Saree was nine. Kaleigh came to Saree's house all the
time.

One day Saree was sad. Kaleigh said, "What's wrong
Saree?"

Saree said, "I'm moving."

"Where?" Kaleigh shouted.

"To Panama City, Florida," Saree moaned. Their best
friend relationship was over. Saree didn't want to go, but she
had to.

The next day Saree zoomed to Kaleigh's house on her bike
and rang the doorbell. Kaleigh answered the door. Saree had
a wide smile on her face and shouted, "I'm not moving! My
parents thought about how we've been best friends and said
we're not moving!"

"Yeah!" yelled Kaleigh.

A couple of years pass. Kaleigh is eighteen; Saree is
seventeen. They're out of college and best friends.

A few years later, Kaleigh and Saree had a fight. They
were yelling and pulling hair just because they were lied to and
told something not true.

They started their jobs. Kaleigh's was in singing, and
Saree's was in singing and soccer. They still enjoyed a lot of
things together. Their lives were going so great until Kaleigh
got very sick. Saree tried to help, but she got sick, too. They
were so sick that they died. Their graves are right next to each
other. Saree's grave is covered with her trophies; Kaleigh's is
covered with her singing trophies.

Every day, people look and see all of Saree's trophies
and all of Kaleigh's trophies. Some cry. One little girl said,
"They're in heaven now. They're safe and hanging out with
each other and alive."

PS – Saree and Kaleigh were really in heaven

The Roadrunner Dash
Taylor D.
Ms. Elmer, 4th Grade

One day, a boy named Taylor and his roadrunner, Speedy, entered a roadrunner dash. Speedy had one small green feather on top of his head. On June 25 they went to the dash. The other roadrunners were older than Speedy. The referee shot a gun up in the air. The roadrunners shot off to a blazing start. Taylor rooted for Speedy.

The first mile of the race was in a desert. Speedy was in last place until a giant crack opened up in the ground. One roadrunner tripped and fell. Speedy passed him. Speedy flew through the first mile.

The second mile of the race was a stormy dirt road. The dirt got wet and Speedy slipped. He got up, still pushing on. A lightning bolt struck the roadrunner in front of him.

The final mile was up a volcano and across the lava. Speedy and the champion, Fire Foot, were the only roadrunners left. They blazed up the volcano. When they got to the top, Speedy and Fire Foot were neck and neck. They jumped over the boiling lava pit and ran down the volcano to the finish line. Speedy and Fire Foot dashed for the finish line. It was a photo finish! They looked at the picture. Speedy had won by a certain small green feather. Speedy and Taylor then went home.

Mark and His Snake
Brady C.
Mrs. Partain, 4th Grade

Mark had a snake named Biff. One day Mark took Biff to school. He had the snake in a bag which he put in his locker. At recess, Mark looked in the locker, and the bag was still there, but Biff was not. Then the school got put on lockdown, and the police had to come to the school to catch the snake. They caught it and Mark took it home.

The Zombie Attack
Trent B.
Ms. Elmer, 4th Grade

One day Zack, Logan, Austin, Holden, and I were playing hide and seek. Holden was counting while Austin hid in the bathroom. Logan and I hid under the bed. Zack hid in a closet. He pulled down a rope then a pile of underwear fell on his head.

When Holden was finished counting, they heard Austin scream. "AAAAHHHH!!!!"

Holden said, "Here over here."

Logan, Zack, and I ran to the base. Still Zack had underwear on him. Holden said, "What's wrong?"

"ZOMBIE!" Austin said. "Zombie behind you!" Holden turned around and punched his head off.

"Look out the window! Zombies!" we called to the army. They came to win the war. We looked over and saw Chase, Grant and Justin dressed like zombies so they won't get bitten by one. They gave us guns. We fought until grandma said, "Who wants pancakes?" The war was done. We won and you know Josh was King of Zombies.

A Day at the Beach
Bralynn C.
Ms. Williams, 4th Grade

This was going to be the hottest day this summer so we are going to the beach! "Hooray!" I shout. We are about to leave so I go pack.

We are now of the road but now I'm on the edge of my seat. I play my DS a little. I sing a little. I squirm, wiggle, and dance in my seat.

"We are here," Dad said. I jumped out of my seat.

"Yeah!" I screamed. The whole park heard. I put on my swimsuit. When I was done my mom and dad had already set up. I ran to the water. SPLASH! I jumped in. I stood there for a moment. Brrr! I thought. "I'll get used to it," I said shaking. I went back with my mom. I watched as the sea sparkled. I went back in the water.

"Time to go!" Dad said.

I knew today would be the best day ever!

Summer School
Gracen B.
Ms. Williams, 4th Grade

Brrriiiingggg! Yes!! School's out for the summer!
"Alli can you stay for a minute?" asked Mrs. Blake.
"Ok. Sure!" I said.
"Honey, you have made good grades all year and all but your parents think you need to go to summer…"
I cut her off. "Summer school!"
"Yes, sweetie. It was my choice," Mrs. Blake said with a frown.
No matter what this summer, I was going to summer school. My parents wouldn't talk about it.
"Mom, dad why do I have to go to summer school?" I asked.
All they said was, "Because you do."
After one week of summer school I got kicked out because I was making such good grades. Mom tried to get me back in but the school said no. Yes! No more summer school. Just kick back and relax for the rest of the summer.

The Friendly Dinosaur
Brady W.
Mrs. Partain, 4th Grade

One day, Emily went into her backyard with her brother Alan. She was surprised to see a huge, green dinosaur in the garden. "It's a T-Rex!" exclaimed Emily.
"Yes, and it's eating mother's geraniums," Alan replied.
So, they went and told their Dad, and he got a baseball bat and went to the garden with them. The dinosaur came over to their Dad, and he got ready to swing, but it turned out it was a nice dinosaur. It began to lick their Dad! Then it licked the kids. It then put its tail down and let the kids climb up, and the dinosaur began walking around with them. When the kids asked him to stop, he did, and they got down. They named him Alex, and they were best friends from then on.

The Tricky Genie
Caleb C.
Mrs. Partain, 4th Grade

Phyllis found an old bottle at the beach. There was a cork in it. When Phyllis pulled out the cork, a genie popped out of the bottle. "Greetings young mortal. Your wish is my command," said the genie.

Phyllis then began thinking of what she could wish for. It was around breakfast time so she said, "I wish for a hot pancake!"

The genie said, "Okay," and a pancake fell on her face. The genie said, "You should have wished for a pancake on a plate!"

Then Phyllis said, "Next, I wish for a million dollars!" The next thing she knew she was being chased by the police and she was forty. She quickly jumped out of the car and went back to the beach. The genie was still there. She said, "I wish I had three more wishes." Then she wished that she was younger, so the genie put her back in her Mother's tummy!" When she was born, her Mom did not want her, so she was shipped to Australia and lived there happily ever after with the kangaroos!

Randy's Day
Danielle A.
Mrs. Partain, 4th Grade

One day Randy was walking down Main Street. A crowd of people ran past. "Run!" one shouted, "Duckzilla is coming!"

"What?" said Randy. "Ah! Hah!"

"What is going on?" asked the duck.

"It IS you," Randy said.

"What?" asked the duck.

Randy replied, "You! You are large and feathery"

"I know, and I love it very much" said the large duck.

"You like that?" asked Randy.

"Yep," replied the duck.

"I would like to be you. I am just a person," sighed Randy.

"Oh no!" exclaimed Randy.

"What?" asked the duck.

"It's the policeeeeeee!" yelled Randy. "Hide."

The policeman asked, "Have you seen a large duck?"

"No I have not," stated Randy.

"Whew, that was close," said the duck.

"Yep. Well, I have to go home. My family might be worried," Randy said.

"Okay," said the duck. "Bye!"

"Bye" yelled Randy.

How Phyllis Got Her Wish
Joselyn D.
Mrs. Partain, 4th Grade

One day Phyllis went to the beach and found an old bottle on the sand. There was a cork in it. When Phyllis pulled out the cork, a genie popped out of the bottle. "Greetings young mortal," said the genie. "Your wish is my command."

"I thought you were supposed to come out of a lamp," said Phyllis.

"Well," said the genie. "My name is Destiny, and here is my story."

"This mean man caught my lamp and kept it, and then put me in the bottle. Now, here I am. End of story! What is your wish? I have to give you some rules. Rule number one-there is no making you fall in love. Rule number two-no being mean to anyone. Rule number three-no being bad!"

So Phyllis thought of her first wish. She thought and thought and suddenly asked to be grown up. The genie made her a grown up. Her second wish was that she was the richest person in the world. Her third wish was that she was a princess. All of her wishes came true!

My Space Dream and Me
Destiny B.
Mrs. Partain, 4th Grade

Once there was a girl named Destiny Marie B. or Miss
Priss for short. She was one of the richest people in the whole
entire world! One day she was in her fourth grade class with
the best teacher in the whole world. Her name was Mrs.
Partain. They were learning about the solar system, and the
whole day Destiny thought what it would be like if she could
go into space. She dreamed about it the whole day at school,
and when she got home she told her Mom, "I want to go to
outer space."

Her Mom replied, "Oh, my little darling, you're too little."

Destiny cried, "I'm ten years old for crying out loud!"

"That's too bad, " said her Mom. "If you went then your
sisters would want to go too."

"Fine!" Destiny said.

That night she said good night to her sisters and went to
sleep even though she could barely sleep because her sister
Hope was snoring all night and taking all of the covers.
Destiny finally fell asleep about 4:00 A.M. She dreamed that
she was in space. She dreamed that she went to Mars.

There Destiny was in her purple, pink, and blue rocket
ship. Her spacesuit was pink, purple, blue, and fuzzy. She also
had along her little doggy, Bella, dressed in her purple, pink,
and blue suit! Then, all of a sudden there was a big thump!
Bella and Destiny got out of the spaceship. They were finally
on Jupiter. It was so scary. Thump, Bella and Destiny fell into
a wide crater. It was very hard to get out of. They decided
that they were kind of getting board on Jupiter, so Destiny and
Bella jumped to Saturn.

Saturn was so big and pretty. Bella and Destiny ran on
Saturn's rings. She was colorful, and the brightest planet
because of her yellowness. They decided to take a visit on
Uranus.

Destiny and Bella hopped on over to Uranus. Of course it
was very colorful too, but it looked kind of like slime because
it was a bright green color. They decided not to try and run
on the rings because they were going upways. So Destiny and
Bella left Uranus and hopped to Neptune.

Destiny hopped on Neptune and screamed, "Oh my gosh.
It is blue, and blue is one of my favorite colors. This should be
my planet!" Destiny loved it, but she really loved rings, so she

left and danced on the stars to Mars.

Mars was a really small planet, but Destiny liked it. She wondered why it was so windy, and when she walked to the other side, she saw a dust devil. Destiny bounced off Mars and walked on air onto Earth.

"My home planet," Destiny sighed. She kept walking and then she found something. It was a silver space car. Oh my, there is an awful lot of trash in Earth's orbit. It looks like rings. Destiny was so mad that she began to clean it. She cleaned up Earth really fast, and then it looked really pretty again, so she hopped over to Venus.

There she was on Venus. Venus was not a pretty planet because of its colors. Destiny's eyes were hurting because of the light from the sun. She decided to go on over to Mercury.

Mercury was ugly to her too, and it looked burnt. It was a brown planet, and she could not stand the light, so Destiny went to the Milky Way.

Destiny and Bella slipped on their swimsuits and began to swim in the Milky Way. It was fun! There was pink milk in it. Then, Destiny left her dream and woke up.

When Destiny woke up, she was sad that her dream was over. It was the best dream ever!

Larry and His Father Go To Space
Hope B.
Mrs. Partain, 4th Grade

Larry's father, Professor Carson, was a scientist. One day Larry visited his father in the laboratory. "What's that machine?" asked Larry.

"It's a time machine," said Professor Carson. "All I have to do is push this button, and it can take us anywhere in time and space!"

"Wow!" said Larry. "Let's go!"

"Okay," said Professor Carson.

So they took off and went into space and ran into moon rocks floating around and a lot more, but then it was time for Larry to go to bed. They went down to Earth, and they went to sleep. Larry said, "I love you Dad." And his Dad said it back.

In the morning, Larry and his Dad were at the computer looking up things like other planets and then Larry asked, "Will the sun ever crash into our Earth?"

His Dad said, "It could, but that's a million years from now."

Together, Larry and his Dad did a lot more research on space.

The Magic Trip Through The Solar System
Kayley R.
Mrs. Partain, 4th Grade

Hi, my name is Kayley. It's the first day of school, and right as I walk in, I know this isn't going to be a normal school year! I find my desk, and just as I sit down, Mrs. Partain starts talking about a report on the solar system. Everyone is very upset about having to do a report on the first day of school. Then she announces that we are going on a field trip to help us understand the solar system. Everyone is astonished! We get everything we need and go to the bus. We all wonder where we are going.

We are all on the bus, and the engine starts to rumble. We look out the window to see the bus begin to grow rockets. Then we blast off into space. Everyone wants to go to the moon, and we get there in like four minutes. Everyone is in a hurry to get out, but then we remember that there is no air, and everyone is disappointed. Then, Mrs. Partain pushed a button and pink, purple, blue, and green space suits come down within our reach. We all got our equipment and headed out of the hatch. A hatch is something that you use to get in and out of vehicles.

When on the moon, all of the students started leaping and shouting with joy. Suddenly we heard a loud thud. Austin, a boy in my class, had tripped and fell over a small space rover. A space rover is a small device that scientists use to take pictures of planets or the moon. Austin got up and wasn't injured. After that, everyone just stayed away from the rover. Later, we got back on the spaceship and decided that we wanted to go to Mars. Mars is known as the red planet because of the red color that its rusty soil gives off.

Once we reached Mars, we all got out and heard some music. We decided to follow it. We followed the sound all the way to a Milk Shake Shop. We walked in and there were aliens! All of the aliens saw us and said, "Hi!" After that, they offered us lunch and a milkshake. We took it gladly. After lunch, we decided to go to just one more planet. We all decided on Saturn. We could not wait to see Saturn's pretty rings.

When we came into Saturn's view, we unbuckled our seatbelts to look out of the windows. As we did, we floated up into the air. We all began laughing and playing. What I know about good old gravity is that each planet has its own gravity.

In space there is no gravity, so that is why you float.

After laughing and floating around for awhile, we grabbed onto the windows and caught one final glimpse of Saturn. As we were headed home, Myla, another student in my classroom, noticed a big black hole in space. Mrs. Partain told us that it was just a black hole. A black hole is a hole in space with extreme gravitational pull. If you get sucked into it, you are not coming back. We wisely chose to stay clear of it.

After awhile we saw Earth. Mrs Partain yelled for us to hang on . In minutes we entered the atmosphere and were back at school.

Back in the classroom, Mrs. Partain told us about another field trip that we were taking to the planetarium. We all signed with relief. This was just a start to an unusual school year with Mrs. Partain

My Magic Dog Lily
Mallory A.
Mrs. Partain, 4th Grade

One day I woke up and my Mom yelled upstairs, "Mallory, take Lily for a walk."

I yelled, "Okay!"

I got out of bed, put on my clothes, and then went downstairs. When I took Lily out of her cage, she looked like she floated a little bit, but I thought that she probably just jumped because she was excited. When I took her outside, she was actually floating. She took me away into the air. She took me on a plane. She actually took me on the top of a plane! I was outside for a couple of hours. My Mom got worried. She looked in the backyard. I was not there.

I liked flying with Lily, so I shouted,"Whoo! Hoo!"

My Mom thought it was some kid down the street. She was so worried that she called the police. When the police got to our house, they started to investigate. One cop just looked up into the sky. He saw Lily and me. He was confused. He yelled, "Hello, are you Lily and Mallory?"

I answered, "Yes!"

He replied, "You need to come down here right now!"

My Mom came outside and yelled, "Ya'll scared me. Come down here now!"

So, Lily and I fell down. I landed in the cops arms! Lily landed in my Mom's arms. The cop put me down. I ran to my

Mom and hugged her so tight. My Mom said, "I never knew Lily was magic."

I said, "I never knew Lily was magic either, but she's very special."

We were both happy. We had a magic dog! We went inside and had some lunch with the cops.

My Adventures
Myla L.
Mrs. Partain, 4th Grade

My name is Myla. I love doing fun things, but it was cold and snow was coming. It came really fast. My brother Hunter and I got on a sled and slid on it, but the cold was going away and it did not last for long. It was getting warm. When it is warm, we go camping. I asked my Mom about it on a Saturday, and she said, "We are going today."

My Mom and Dad fixed up the camper, and I put my puppy in her cage. She was going with us. When we were all ready, my Nana came and my brother and I got into her car. She always comes camping with us. When we got there, I wanted to go fishing, so my Nana and I went fishing. I caught some fish, and she did too. When we were done, I went up to the campsite and played with my puppy Sugar. At night, we roasted marsh mellows, and they were good. When it was time to go, I was sad, but I had fun. Later, when we got home, it was so relaxing that I went to bed.

A week later my Mom said it was time for softball to start. I went to practice, and it was so much fun. I went for a while. Three months later it was time again to go to the mountains. We packed the car and took off. When we got there, I went to panning for gold. We found little bitty pieces of gold. We also went horseback riding. My horse's name was Mingo, and my Mom was on a slow horse named Pearl. My Dad rode the fast horse that was named Roach! My Nana's horse just hung out with Pearl. His name was Arab, and Hunter's horse was named Tony. The person who led us had a horse named Buck.

Later on another vacation, we went to the beach for five days. It was so much fun. My Mom even bought me a squishy toy and my brother a truck. We swam a lot, and we went to the doughnut store and got some doughnuts. I love the beach! It was so much fun. When our five days were over, we went back home. My Mom then told us that we were going to go to the

North Carolina mountains!

A week passed and we headed to the mountains. My Dad and I climbed a mountain! When we got back to our car, we just headed home. I really thought that my trips were over, but the next day, he asked me if I wanted to go hunting! I said, "Yes!"

My Dad and I went hunting, and even though we did not see anything, it was fun. When we got home, we told my Mom all about it. I just love doing fun things!

A Wacky Day
Summer C.
Mrs. Partain, 4th Grade

One day Penny went into her backyard with her sister, Amber. She was surprised to see a huge, three horned dinosaur in the garden. "It's a T-Rex," Penny exclaimed.

"Yes, and it's eating Mother's geraniums," Amber replied.

"I thought they were extinct," said Penny.

"So did I," explained Amber.

They were both terrified, no doubt. They wanted to go inside, but somehow they both didn't. The T-Rex wasn't really doing anything mean or wrong other than eating the geraniums.

"It looks like it wants to play," said Amber.

"Yeah, it does look like it wants to play," said Penny.

"He's not acting vicious at all. He's acting really nice," said Amber.

"I guess we can play with him," said Penny.

"Alright," Amber said scaredly.

The T-Rex was actually really nice to the girls.

"He's really fun to play with," said Penny.

"Yeah, and he's not vicious at all," replied Amber.

"He certainly is the nicest dinosaur that I've ever even heard of," said Penny.

Just then the dinosaur lifted them up and took them on a walk through the city. As soon as the girls got home, the T-Rex just disappeared. They were so sad, but they realized that they had just had the best day of their lives. They both said at the same time, "Wow, this was the best day ever!"

The Hole and the Old Ghost Man
Rebekah O.
Ms. Cochran, 5th Grade

Rebekah, Isabella, and their dog Max could hear the whistle of a faraway train. It made the night seem even scarier, because it was Halloween. They started trick-or-treating at around 5:00. A few hours later when they reached the last house, they could barely hold their buckets. Then they heard someone call them saying, "I don't believe you got your candy here yet."

Isabella and Rebekah's mom, Claire came and picked them up. Max was so nervous he could barely even walk! Right before we got in the car, Max smelled something in the woods. Then seconds later, he bolted into the forest. Poor Rebekah and Isabella had to chase after him. When they finally caught up to him they realized he was barking at an old man. Then the old man took off deeper into the woods. Good thing Rebekah got Max onto his leash in time. Although Isabella had a good grip on his leash, he still broke free. Once again, Rebekah and Isabella dashed after him.

After a while, Isabella had thought that they were seriously lost when they saw a glimpse of the old man. Obviously Rebekah saw him too because she started to run after him. While they were running they heard something dart behind them. They quickly turned around to find Max trying to keep up. Out of nowhere they fell into an extremely deep hole in the ground as they watched the old man disappear. They were trying and trying but they just couldn't get out! A minute later the hole closed up! Surely at this point they were all scared.

At the same time, Claire was looking for them. Hours later she decided to call Search and Rescue. When they arrived she told them, "I couldn't find them anywhere. It is like they disappeared."

Later one of the men from Search and Rescue came back and said, "We haven't found any signs yet." The search was on for days. After the eighth day Claire was ready to quit.

While Isabella was trying to find food, Rebekah was trying to find resources, and Max was taking a nap. They were all trying to survive. Later Rebekah tried to pick Max up, but he was too heavy. Isabella was watching her when she realized there was a trap door under Max. She pointed the door out to Rebekah, and they tried to pull it open. Once they got it open, they found a bed, food, and a place to play around. It wasn't clean, but at least they found it.

Two weeks later, Rebekah, Isabella, and Max were found. Claire couldn't believe the story about the hole, but what choice did she have? So every year when it comes time to trick-or-treating, they stay home and just hand out the candy. So the lesson you were supposed to learn was to stay safe on Halloween.

A Day at the Fire Station with Captain Bryce
Douglas D.
Ms. Cochran, 5th Grade

Bryce is on his way to the fire station. It is where he works for 24 hours. He spends 24 hours with his fire station family. Then he os off for 48 hours to be with his family at home. Bryce is the captain of fire station #7. He has to make sure that his crew and the equipment is ready for a fire.

Just after breakfast, they have to spring into action! There is a fire at a house. The dispatch gives them the address. Everyone gets their gear on quickly! Captain Bryce rides in the front seat of the pumper truck. The pumper truck holds 1,000 gallons of water to use at the water. They use the lights and the sirens to get to the fire as fast as they can to try to save the house. Captain Bryce tells Michael to get the hose and pump some water on the house. The ambulance arrives too in case anyone is hurt. The ladder truck arrives after the ambulance. The ladder can go up 100 feet.

Captain Bryce wants his crew to go into the house to fight the fire. The other firemen are afraid the roof is going to cave in on them. Captain Bryce and Brian turn on their air, get an axe, and the hose. They go into the house. The house is very hot and dark. There is a lot of fire around them. They hear a girl screaming. She is screaming "HELP!!" They follow her screams to a bedroom. They knock the door down to get her. Captain Bryce and Brian grab the girl. They are glad she closed the door when the fire started because it helped keep the fire away from her. The girl tells them her name is Haleigh. They share their air with Haleigh to keep the smoke away from her. They break the window in the bedroom to get out. There are bars over the window. They cannot get out of the house. Firefighters Myriah and Makala climb the ladder on the ladder truck. They use their tools to cut the bars on the window. They take Haleigh from Captain Bryce and Brian. They carry her down the ladder.

EMT Rick checks to make sure that Haleigh is okay. As Captain Bryce and Brian are climbing into the ladder, there was a big BOOM! Captain Bryce got burned as he climbed out of the window. Captain Bryce will be okay. All the firefighters work together to put out the rest of the fire. They go back to the fire station. They still have to clean the tools and the fire trucks. They also have to get showers to clean off the dirt and the smoke.

They missed their lunch while they were at the fire. They got to eat dinner. After dinner they watched TV and then went to bed. They got to sleep all night. They did not get a call. The next morning Captain Bryce ate breakfast at the station. He is going to an elementary school to teach the students about fire safety. He tells them that if they are on fire, they need to STOP, DROP, and ROLL. He tells them that their families need a fire escape plan in case they had a fire at their home. He eats lunch on his way home. He finally gets to go home and see his family. They are happy to see him!

The Ghost Bus
Jordan W.
Mrs. Griffis, 5th Grade

If you ride a new bus to school and it's a bad bus, usually it has a mean bus driver or there is a bully or two. The new bus I had to ride recently was way different! I will begin my story with the conversation between John and I.

"Hey Jordan, that math test was hard wasn't it?" asked John.

"Yes, it was," I replied. My friend John usually asks about tests when we go home every day.

"Jordan, are you riding the bus home?" asked John.

"Yes, but I'm riding a new bus. Bus 98-2," I replied.

"Never heard of it. Well, see you later," John said.

"Bye," I replied. After I was finished telling John goodbye, I took a look at this new bus I was riding. It looked like it was in a bad accident, but I just climbed on board. When I looked at the bus driver I noticed he was pale and had holes and cuts in his shirt and pants. I didn't want to be rude so I just took my seat.

I sat next to a kid who had shredded up clothes and cuts on his face. "Hi, my name is Dylan. What's yours?"

"Jordan," I replied. "Hey, I don't mean to be rude, but how did you get those cuts? Were you in some sort of accident?" I asked.

"Yes," he replied.

"Oh, do you go to this school?" I asked.

"I used to," he answered.

"What do you mean, 'used to'?" I asked nervously. "Well, this is my stop, Dylan," I yelled as I was jumping from the bus.

Dylan yelled back, "I wouldn't count on it." I wondered what he meant as I checked the mail. When I turned around to watch the bus drive away, it just faded away. Well, that was weird. I walked into my house reading the headline of the newspaper, and it said that bus number 98-2 had crashed. Everyone on board was reported DEAD at the scene. That means all of the people on the bus that I just rode were DEAD! Except me.

Queen Hailey and King Justin live Happily Ever After.
Reanna W. and Haley A.
Mrs. Griffis, 5th Grade

Once upon a time there was a girl who fell in love with a boy named Prince Justin. She was a little small town girl named Hailey, and she had a desire to marry Prince Justin. She went to see Prince Justin so that she could ask him to marry her. She said, "Hi, I am Hailey. I came to ask you to marry me."

Prince Justin accepted her proposal saying," Yes I would love to marry you." The next day they got married. Upon being married, Prince Justin became the King and Hailey was his Queen. On their honeymoon King Justin was walking along the beach when a evil witch popped up. Suddenly the evil witch put an evil spell on the new king, and it turned the prince into a frog. The king got to a mirror and saw that he was a frog. Meanwhile Queen Hailey was dreaming when she suddenly awoke in the middle of a nightmare wondering where King Justin could be. She jumped out of bed and ran outside looking for King Justin.

So the next day Queen Hailey was worrying. Then, she found a frog and thought that it sounded like King Justin.

Queen Hailey said, "How can I turn you back into a King?" They both went to their castle and tried to figure out how to change the frog back to King Justin.

Meanwhile they were sitting in the royal library reading about spells when Queen Hailey exclaimed, "I found one! It says if a spell has you turned into something the only way to change you back is to kiss your true love at the stroke of midnight."

"Well, that is easy you are my true love," King Justin proclaimed.

So on that very night at the stroke of midnight the frog turned back to the handsome, charming king he had always been. Queen Hailey and King Justin were happy and very wealthy.

They lived Happily Ever After.

The Sewer
Robyn L.
Mrs. Griffis, 5th Grade

One day my best friend, Jessica, and I were playing at her house. We were building piles of leaves and jumping in them. Then, we came across a sewer. The metal grate read, "Est. 1892."

"Wow," we both exclaimed.

"Where do you think it leads to?" asked Jessica.

"There's only one way to find out," I replied. So we both pulled with all our might and opened it up. It seemed like it weighed a ton.

"Oh, my gosh!" we both cried.

"What is that?" I said. "I think it is ..... a skeleton. Ahh!" I screamed.

"Hey, what is that in its hand?" Jessica said. "It looks like a leash. That must mean there is a dog in here somewhere. Let's go check it out."

"Ya think I really want to do that?" I asked.

"Okay now, come on," she pleaded.

"Wait, what if there are snakes, rats, or alligators?" I said stalling.

Impatiently she said, "There's not!"

"Okay, if you say so."

We had been in there for thirty minutes ~ the most terrifying thirty minutes of my life. I was so scared. Even though Jessica didn't act scared, I think she was just as freaked out as I was. "Have you seen the dog yet?" I asked. "It is not alive, so it is going to be hard to find."

Jessica said, "Yea, but what if it is still alive?"

"Well of course it is not alive," I insisted.

"Well, I think it is," said Jessica. "Let's keep look for that dog."

"Man, how big is this place?" I wondered aloud.

"Look I see some water ahead," screamed Jessica as she ran ahead. "Ahhhh!" was all I could hear as Jessica vanished.

"Jessica," was all that came out of my mouth as a I screamed bloody murder. "Where are you?" I finally managed to get out. I suddenly saw Jessica right ahead of me. We were both sliding down a broken pipe.

"Robyn?" Jessica screamed.

"Yea?" I responded is a somewhat relieved voice.

When we came to a sudden stop at the end of the pipe, Jessica calmly said, "We made it. Now back to looking for that dog." That is when we heard the sound. Ruff, ruff. It couldn't be. There was just no way a dog could have lived that long. "No way," Jessica said. RRRRarfff! We heard him again. "Follow it," Jessica said. We ran like a monkey chasing its bananas trying to catch that dog.

"What!" we exclaimed as we reached the source of the sounds. "It is just a record player."

"Then what is that?" we both said at the same time. For just beyond the record player stood the dirtiest dog I have ever seen.

We ran over to it as Jessica asked, "What breed is it?"

"It looks like a mutt to me," I answered. "So that dog was alive after all. Wait, look, this dog has a leash." (What do you think?)

We climbed back out of the sewer and brought the dog home for a nice warm bath and tasty bowl of dog food. Later we told our friend, Caitlynn, about our adventure. She could hardly believe our story.

The Elf Named Cassie
Sarah H.
Mrs. Griffis, 5th Grade

Once upon a time there was an elf; her name was Cassie. Cassie was also good at magic. She WAS magic!

"Rose!" Cassie yelled.

"Sorry Cassie. I'm practicing my spell casting," Rose explained.

Rose was one of Cassie's good friends. Then they had a spell that went wrong... "Nice, now look what you did," exclaimed Rose.

"Oops," was all Cassie could think to say.

"Cassie, you better fix this!" Rose said. Cassie responded angrily asking Rose if she wanted her help or not. "Yes! How are we supp- Oh my goodness, C-c-cassie," Rose stuttered.

"What? Why do you have that look? Ahhh!" Cassie yelled with horror. "Rose, help me!"

"Caaaassssie!!" Rose yelled. "Edge of me go into you, but in return you give your soul."

Suddenly Cassie rose up into the air and repeated that line, "Edge of me go into you, but in return you give your soul."

"Cassie? Rose said.

"Ahh!" Rose yelped.

"Rose!" Cassie yelled.

"Cassie, are you okay?" Rose asked?

"Quick, get on!" Cassie demanded.

"Okay," Rose complied.

"Great, we're stuck!" Cassie said.

"The horror!" Rose exclaimed.

"Hey, people. Hi, there," a young girl named Caitlynn said.

THUMP! BOOM! POOF!

"Cassie," Rose quivered. "What's going on? Cassie! You w-were floating, and I was s-scared nearly half to death!" Rose said.

"Floating?" Cassie asked.

"Uh-huh," Rose said.

"We need to get out of here, and QUICK!" Cassie exclaimed.

"Why?" asked Rose.

"Can't you see? It is evil here!"

Our New Life in Atlanta
Tess H.
Mrs. Griffis, 5th Grade

The Letter
My eyes flew open. I could smell the fields, lilacs, and those grits Mama said she'd make. I thought to myself, "Davey's gonna be a doctor today." He had worked so hard. He sometimes would stay up 'til the crack of dawn makin' medicines. I half ran to my closet, and I searched through it for what I wanted. Sundress – no, work dress – no, "Ahh Ha!" I said aloud. I had found my Sunday Dress. I thought it would be PERFECT for Davey's graduation. I say next to my friend, and neighbor, Lily. She had just moved here from Florida. She had also called, "The Sunshine State". Weird name, if you ask me. Then, Davey stepped up on the wooden platform. Before he walked toward the professor, he winked and flashed a huge grin my direction. When Davey was handed his Medical Degree, the whole Reed family stood up. Paulina even giggled. We rode home in the wagon, full of smiles, hugs, and high fives. When I walked up the front porch, that's when I saw the letter - the letter with Rosellen Sanders name on it. I quickly opened the letter and read her plea.

> *Dear Reeds,*
> *I have been very sick. I've had a fever. I think*
> *it's Measles. Davey's a doctor, right? Please*
> *help. I'm in Kentucky. Help ~*
> *Rosellen Sanders*

When I finished reading her letter, I ran to Davey. He read the first sentence, then he got up and got his medicine bag. Next, he told us, "C'mon guys, we're going to Kentucky."

Kentucky
"Davey…," Mama began. "How we gonna get there?"
"Easy, I'll drive the wagon," he replied.
"If you say so Son," Mama replied. Jem was bouncier than a catfish in a moon bounce. I ran upstairs to pack my stuff. I packed my sundress and my regular dresses. I also grabbed my book, <u>Anne of Green Gables</u>, by L.M. Montgomery. It was a good book, and it gave me comfort. Just as we sat down in the wagon, Paulina started to cry.
"There, there, it's okay," I cooed. Davey stopped by his

nurse, Scarlet's house.

"Oh my!" she exclaimed when she read the letter. "Of course I'll come." Then all six of us were headed for Kentucky. We passed Tennessee's banjo players, South Carolina's roses, and many roads, but we finally made it! Scarlet and Davey ran to the post office.

"Stay here!" Davey commanded.

"Okay," Jem replied. A few moments later they both returned.

"Did you find out where Rosellen lives?" I asked curiously.

"Yep," Davey said. He took a sheet of paper out of his pocket and read aloud her address, "1725 Fable Road, Frankfort, Kentucky."

"Wow, it'll take at least a day to get there," Mama mused quietly.

"Don't worry Davey," I said to break the silence.

"I hope we can get there before...." he trailed off. Then I realized what he meant by that. If we didn't get there in time, Rosellen could die! We had to get there in time, we just had to...

Rosellen

When we pulled up to Rosellen's house, the lanterns weren't lit. Not a good sign. Davey knocked on the door. After the third knock, Mr. Francis Greenwood appeared at the door. I probably made a face, but I didn't care. What was he doing here? I wondered. "Hello, I'm here to see Rosellen Sanders," Davey said politely. When he said that, he sounded like a real doctor.

"Here, this room on the left," Mr. Greenwood answered. When we saw Rosellen, she looked horrible! Her hair was in a messy pony-tail with strands stuck to her face. Her skin was pale, and she was sweaty, but her eyes were still emerald green, sparkly, and gorgeous to look at.

"Oh, Davey!" she breathed in relief. "I didn't think you would make it or even get my letter."

"Well, here I am," he replied. Mr. Greenwood frowned at this exchange. Davey gave her some medicine, kissed her cheek, and then we were leaving.

"Wait," she called weakly. Davey stepped back and looked her way. "Davey, I'm marrying Francis, and I want you to be my best man." When I heard this, my heart broke for Davey. How could she? Davey loved her. Why would he have come if he didn't?

"Rosellen, I don't know…" he told her.
"Please, Davey, for me?"
"Okay, Rosellen," Davey replied softly.

Summer 1865 (by Rosellen)
As I walked down the stairs of the church, every corner
was filled with flowers! Lilacs, roses, and daisies. As I
walked toward the aisle, everyone stood up. It made me blush.
Hannalee was in front of me as my flower girl. In front of her,
were Jem and Paulina as my ring bearers. Then next to my
husband-to-be was Davey. Davey was my best friend, and I
knew I could go to him for anything. Today was perfect with
him here. I finally got down to the end of the aisle where
Francis stood smiling at me. He was the one I wanted to spend
the rest of my life with. I was irrevocably in love with him. As
we said our vows, I glanced at Davey to see him smile at me. It
made me sad to think about him, so I quickly snapped my head
around to look at my husband. "Now you may kiss the bride,"
the preacher said. When he said those words, I knew I had a
great life ahead.

A Birthday Wish
Reanna W.
Mrs. Griffis, 5th Grade

Reanna was so excited for her birthday. She did not want
much. She wanted one thing, and that was a pet. She had no
pets at home, just her old dog that did not want to play. She
wanted a puppy. She had so many names for a pet. She was
prepared to take care of it, but the bad thing was that her
parents did not have a lot of money. She didn't have a lot of
hope, but she did have some.
The next morning was her birthday. She woke to the
smell of her favorite food - pancakes and bacon. She asked
what they were doing today. They said, "We are going to sing
happy birthday, cut the cake, then we are going to go get your
presents." She knew what that meant.
She got ready as fast as she could. She went back
downstairs to sing happy birthday and eat the cake. She jumped
in the car, and they were off. When they pulled up to the animal
shelter she ran as fast as she could to the door.
They went in and saw a lot of cats. No puppies or dogs.
The receptionist said," We haven't had any dogs in here in a

long time." Reanna was speechless. "Sorry," the receptionist said. Reanna felt so sad I think there were tears in her eyes.

Her mom said, "There are more animal shelters in Georgia." So they said their goodbyes to all the cats, and they were off to some other animal shelter.

When the car pulled in, she recognized the shelter. She thought it was where they had rescued their old dog. They walked in, and everybody was so inviting. They said that they haven't seen them since their old dog's check up. They asked, "What can we do for you?" She told them that it was her birthday, and she was there for a puppy. "Well, we have an enormous selection of puppies. But I think I know one that you will fall in love with. We found her mother with seven puppies on the side of the road. But out of those seven I know one that is just like you. She was the runt of the litter."

They took Reanna to the cages, and she saw this one puppy that was the right one for her. She told her mom, and she said "I like that one too." So they got the puppy and brought it to its new home. She named her new puppy Morgan; it was a girl puppy. She got her birthday wish this year. She is now very happy with Morgan and her family. Next year her birthday wish might be to get Morgan a sister or brother.

Dreams really do come true.

Frankenstein
Rose H.
Mrs. Griffis, 5th Grade

The night before Halloween there was a haunted house. It was filled with monsters. The haunted house was really scary to other people. Little babies did not like the haunted house at all, but big kids like it a lot. There were not scared, or at least they acted like they weren't. Adults did not like it, either. However, that night it got scarier and scarier. Something was changing, and I had a feeling no one would like it after all of these changes began to take place.

Caitlynn was about to go into the house for a scary adventure when out of the house came a terrifying monster. "It w-w-was Frankenstein," stuttered Caitlyn as she trembled in fear. Caitlynn was so scared; she did not like the haunted house anymore. Frankenstein did not like anyone, not big kids, not babies, no one! All of the big kids that were getting a little too scared in the house wanted out, but Frankenstein would not let them out. No matter what they tried, they could not get out. He stood at the door and kept watch on the only way in and out of the house.

The kids stood inside and screamed and cried in terror, but he only laughed at them. Many of the kids wondered, "Will we ever escape?" It was a long, terrifying night for them. However, when daylight hit, Frankenstein vanished. The kids were so relieved to be out of the house, they never again asked their parents to let them go to a haunted house.

Kirklon and the Friendship
Karee' C.
Mrs. Griffis, 5th Grade

There once was a boy named Kirklon, and he wanted some more friends because he hung out with the same people all the time. Everyday Kirklon got out of bed, got dressed, and got on the bus. He always sat in the same seat on the bus and always sat by the same people. Kirklon really wanted a change in his life. Then he met me. I'm not saying he was boring or anything, but he had a lot more fun when I came into his life.

Now, he goes to Mason's house and all that and never seems to have time for the friend that really helped him to meet new people. Do you think I was better off not getting him help with making new friends? Should I have let him continue not living life to the fullest? I would ask him, but I think he is not good at those kinds of things. Do you know what I mean? He can't really open up as easily as I do. I mean, like if you ask me to tell you something that you know I want to share, I will tell you right then and there ~ trust me.

I really sometimes wonder before I go to sleep, "Will I ever get that boy to open up and share his feelings with the world, or only with me?" Maybe, just maybe, he doesn't feel comfortable about me, or maybe he does share his feelings with the world or his other friends sometimes. I just want Kirklon to understand that I am here for him forever and always. If he never shares his feelings with me then that's kind of his loss, because I am known to be an excellent listener and problem solver.

Let me know what you think, just talk to the paper right now. Go to a place where you have complete peace and serenity. No, I asked you, if you helped someone meet lots of new friends and gave them what they wanted, would you want them to share their feelings with you?

Personally, I do not know what I would do if the shoe was on the other foot. I guess Kirklon is fine with both, because I have heard and seen some things that he never tells me. Actually, to tell you the truth, he doesn't really talk to me at all anymore. I do miss him talking to me though. I miss his smile. He just has this amazing smile that will make anyone feel better even if the world was about to end. I honestly do not think that Kirklon knows how much I care about him. I just hope that someday he will notice.

The Waiting Christmas Tree
Karee' C.
Mrs. Griffis, 5th Grade

There once was a little girl named Karee'; that's me. My father and I just absolutely loved Christmas! It was December fifth when I wanted to put the Christmas tree up. My daddy said maybe we could do it next Friday, and I got very frustrated. While my mom, Khadijah, shopped for Christmas presents, I decided to go to a Christmas celebration ball with my best friends: Reanna, Samantha, Laura, and Destiny.

I had wanted Kirklon to come also, but he "accidentally" came down with a case of "I don't want to go with you." I still had fun at the ball celebrating with all of my friends. My big brother, Elijah, came and took me back home. He said only one friend could return home with me, so I chose Reanna.

When Reanna, Elijah, and I returned, my mom was already finished buying the presents for my family in New Jersey. Mommy wanted us to help her wrap all of the presents. Reanna got blue, sparkly wrapping paper with pink colored stars on the bottom, Elijah got green, glowing wrapping paper with little puppies all over it, and I used pink wrapping paper with different color peace signs scattered over it. We finally finished wrapping presents after two hours of long, hard, tiring work.

My dad returned home from work shortly after we finished. I begged and pleaded with him to put up the Christmas tree. He told me, "Christmas tree in five minutes!" I was beside myself with excitement, so I had to tell Reanna.

She was like, "Awesome, may I help?"

I replied, "Sure!" as I went on my laptop to update my friends and family on Facebook. I changed my status to read,

"Christmas tree in five minutes."

The five minutes seemed to creep by, until finally I heard my dad's voice. "Karee', I'm sorry, but we are going to have to wait until next Friday to put up our tree."

I cried, "WHATT!!!!!!!" as my wait began again for the Waiting Christmas Tree.

Captain America
Cory C.
Ms. Livermont,5th Grade

"Sir, do you have any information on the missing kids?"

The detective said, "No." But the man was wrong. He did know information for her was the Bandit. Five minutes before the detective left the house Bandit left a note on the car. "Meet me at the border."

As the detective drove by, a kid screamed "3:00pm, 3:00am!"

"What do you want Bandit?"

"I want my life back. I'm a demon. What do you think I want?"

As he ran away the detective said, "Call Captain America!"

As Captain America raced over, he said, "Let's do it!" They both raced to each other to engage in battle. But Bandit knew that to fight a bandit you have to fight this way: you have to fight in the thief way.

"What? But the hero code states that a hero cannot fight in that way," Captain America said. "Fine. I will fight, but if I win you have to go to the cops."

"What if I win?" Bandit asked.

"I will become your apprentice," Captain America said.

As they started the fiery gates of the Underworld rose, but there was a line in-between the Underworld and Heaven. Two men came out. It was the Devil and the Lord.

The Lord said, "You two are champions, Captain America and Bandit. You two will represent Heaven and Underworld."

The two representatives sealed the deal then the battle began. The two clashed, punched, kicked, and stabbed. But only one could win. As the battle continued one took the first fall but they were evenly matched. Then they were blessed with element weapons. As the weapons clashed together they both weakened from one hit.

"I'm not going down yet!" Bandit said.

"I'm not either Bandit, and you're not going to win this fight," Captain America said. "Bring it!"

Blood was spilled but they kept fighting. They have one way to finish the fight. It is to take a shot for the heart! As they threw their weapons at the same time their hearts pumped faster than lightning. But then their blood dropped but two men died that day. Captain America and Bandit!!

The Gods' deal was broken and not either one of them became a god.

The Fishing Trip
Bailey L.
Mrs. Griffis, 5th Grade

It was early in the morning when my pawpaw and I went fishing. We arrived at the lake around 7:30 a.m. while there was still dew on the ground. We unloaded the boat and got the fishing poles and tackle boxes and put them in the boat. Once we got the boat into the icy water, we stepped in.

My pawpaw was the first one to catch a fish. About thirty minutes later, I got a bite. I started reeling it in, the fish was heavy I thought my pole would break. Finally, about five minutes later, I hauled the large mouth into the boat. We put the fish in the floor of the boat until we could make it back to the dock. When we got back to the dock, we cut my line and put a large hook in the fish's mouth. We tied a rope to the hook and tied the rope to the dock. This is where we left my fish when we returned to the lake to do some more fishing.

As soon as I threw my line in the lake, I got another bite. This fish was easy to reel in. We threw the fish back, because it was a baby. My pawpaw and I started back to the dock. When we got there we thought the fish was gone, but then he finally surfaced. We loaded the boat up and got my monster fish. My pawpaw had to use the huge cooler to hold my fish. We put some water in the cooler so my fish would not die. He said we would get this fish mounted so I could hang it on my wall.

I waited day after day to get the fish. I thought the day would never come when I would see my prized fish again. Then, one day when my pawpaw came home from work I saw the fish. It was the greatest thing I have ever seen. It was mounted on a piece of drift wood with a hook in its mouth with a line tied to it. I could not wait to hang it on the wall. My dad finally hung the fish on my wall. It looked great! I will always have that fish as a reminder of that special day of fishing with my pawpaw.

That was the last time I went fishing with my pawpaw. A year after that he got cancer. He would be in and out of the hospital all the time. When he was not in the hospital, he was out on the lake fishing.

Chapter 6
Research

Rattlesnakes
Alexis P.
Ms. Scarbrough, 3rd Grade

Rattlesnakes are very cool to look at. It is yellow, brown, and black with diamonds on its back. They're 18 inches to 46 centimeters long and they grow to 5 feet or 15 meters. They move side to side. It makes a rattle sound with its tail.

Rattlesnakes have a cool habitat. They hide under bunches of places to keep cool. They live in the Piedmont in the woods. If they have old fangs, they grow longer.

When they sleep they curl up. They sleep in burrows where other animals don't and under bushes. They eat whenever they find their food. They snap at it when they want to eat. They eat rats, mice, birds, and lizards.

They can have 5-20 babies at a time. They're born in eggs. Both parents don't take care of them. The babies weigh 85 grams and are 12 centimeters or 30 inches long. They can take care of themselves right away.

They can't hear their own rattle. Their venom can cure diseases. This animal is dangerous. It does not live by people. It cleans up the world.

Raccoons
Krista B.
Ms. Hurndon, 3rd Grade

Do you want to learn facts about raccoons? Well, I did and I want to tell you all about raccoons. Raccoons are gray and have a lot of fur. It weighs about 2 to 3 pounds. He walks on four legs it makes a loud wailing sound.

Well, come into the raccoon's habitat. You will find them in North and South America. They communicate with other raccoons by using a very loud noise. Their habitat is in the woods. They have trees, rocks, and of course the ground.

If you are camping, do not leave food out because raccoons might come and eat it. They eat everything. They eat eggs, seeds, insects, and fish. They catch food by using their long fingers. They mostly eat at night.

Now, let's move on to learn about raccoons and their babies. They do not lay eggs. They have live babies. Raccoons are mammals and mammals do not lay eggs. Baby raccoons stay with their mother for about a year. It really starts to get bigger in one month.

People do not think that raccoons are important but they really are.

Snakes
Jeannine L.
Ms. Elmer, 4th Grade

If you like snakes, you should read this story! This story has a lot of information about snakes!

The first snake I'm going to tell you about is a Rattlesnake. Now, haven't you ever wondered why the Rattlesnake makes that rattling noise? Well, I did. So, I'm going to tell you why! The Rattlesnake's mercury sound comes from its rattle tail; the rattle tail is composed of a series of hollow beads which are actually modified scales from the tail's tip. The rattling occurs when the snake is threatened.

Are Rattlesnakes poisonous? Rattlesnakes are the cause of over seven thousand painful bites a year, but there are only nine or ten deaths a year by those bites. The deadliest venom is from the Mojave and the Tiger Rattlesnakes, but there are not a lot of these bites at all. More bites occur in North Carolina, Arkansas, Texas, and Georgia than any of the other states in America. That's all I know about Rattlesnakes. I hope this will help you.

The next snake I am going to talk to you about is the Viper. The Viper is a very colorful thick-bodied snake. The Viper lives in the rainforest and can also be found in wet places and sometimes in the mountains in small caves. The Viper mainly lives in places that are wet like in the rain forest, woodlands, river banks, bogs, and also in the mountains. This snake can live in many different environments. Their bright colors on their skin help them survive. A bright color usually tells other animals that it is poisonous. The Viper is a very short snake compared to most other snakes. It is 50 to 65 cm long. But the Viper has a very thick body compared to other snakes.

The Viper sometimes has red or brown eyes. Most have yellow skin, but some are green. This color helps the Viper stay camouflaged and hide from its prey. They hang by their tails from a branch and catch their prey in trees. When a bird passes, the Viper hides in the bushes using its camouflage and captures its prey. The snake bite of the Viper is so powerful you would need instant medication or you would lose a lot of blood and die.

The enemies of the Viper would be any type of bird. Birds like to eat small things like snakes, rats, and bugs. Humans are their enemy because their skin is used to make clothes, purses, or shoes. The Viper is an endangered species because of its soft skin. It is so smooth people like to wear it and also keep it for no reason. They are also endangered because they are so interesting and used for dissection by scientists.

The Viper can have a lot of babies! The Viper snake can lay eggs or give birth to live babies depending on what type of Viper it is. Did you know the Viper can lay up to fifty eggs two to three times a year depending on the type of Viper it is? It takes about 50 to 65 days for a Viper egg to hatch depending on the species. A weird fact about the Viper is that the young will stay in the female's mouth until they are well fed by the mother. When the young are ready to come out, they are set free in the wild.

The Viper has a lot of interesting facts. Did you know ancient writings say that the touch of the tongue of a Viper snake healed a person? The viper has a temperature sensing organ in its head.

Well I hope you have learned some more interesting facts about two kinds of snakes because I sure did, and I hope my story has made you interested in looking up some more interesting facts about snakes.

Important People of the Civil War
Griffin L.
Ms. French, 5th Grade

Did you know generals were one of the most amazing people during the Civil War? There were also many brave women during the bloody Civil War. Sherman was a very serious general. Clara Barton was a great nurse who made a huge difference. Grant helped take control of the Confederacy. These people made a huge difference in the Civil War for both the North and the South.

Sherman was a general who went into total warfare. He had a plan to burn Atlanta to the ground. Lincoln hired him because he knew he would get the job done. He also attacked Tennessee, while leading troops to Atlanta. He was admired, but also hated by many southerners.

Clara Barton was a Union nurse. She asked for Medicaid donations. She would go to a battle and give medicine to the wounded. She was asked to start the Red Cross program. The Red Cross is still making a difference today.

General Grant was a very important man for the North. He took over the Mississippi River. He because the Union military leader. He won a battle that made the South surrender at Appomattox Courthouse. Much like Sherman, he was also admired, but feared.

General Sherman, Clara Barton, and General Grant all played parts in this bloody war. The Civil War was one of the most important wars in history because Americans fought against each other. The Civil War was the last war fought on our American soil. The war left its mark in American history forever.

The Civil War
Jack N.
Ms. French, 5th Grade

Do you know much about the Civil War? I'm going to teach you about three important battles. The Battle of Atlanta happened the whole summer of 1864. Attack on Fort Sumter was the first battle in the Civil War. The Battle of Vicksburg started on July 3, 1863. All of these battles changed American history forever.

The Battle of Atlanta started in May 1864. During this battle, the South used the mountains of North Georgia as defenses. At that time, Atlanta held a lot of the South's factories, supplies, and railroads, so the city was important. Even though the South put up a long and great fight, the North won. When the battle was over, General William T. Sherman told President Lincoln that Atlanta was his Christmas gift to him.

The attack on Fort Sumter started April 12, 1861 and it lasted a little longer than a day. This battle happened on the South's territory. This battle happened because Lincoln wouldn't move his troops. The South thought when Lincoln wouldn't move his troops he wanted to start a war. The overall winner of this battle was the South.

The Battle of Vicksburg was a very important battle because the North was fighting for the Mississippi River. The major generals were Ulysses S. Grant and William T. Sherman. In the town of Vicksburg, the South could easily shoot north ships on the Mississippi River. At the town of Vicksburg William T. Sherman surrendered. The overall winner of the battle was the North.

I think these battles were the greatest ones in the war. These battles determined the future of America. It's because of these we are one nation. This nation has become the greatest nation in the world. God bless America!

The Civil War
Austin D.
Ms. French, 5th Grade

Do you know about the brave men in the Civil War? The Civil War was one of the hardest battles for both the North and South. The men gave up their lives to keep us safe. Abraham Lincoln led the Union into battle. Robert E. Lee defeated two Union attacks on Richmond, Va. Ulysses S. Grant led a Union army south from Illinois into Tennessee. Even though they were on opposite sides, these three men played huge parts in the war.

Abraham Lincoln thought slavery was evil. Lincoln did not want to abolish slavery. He wanted to keep slavery from spreading. Lincoln always believed slavery would stop on its own. Lincoln lost the election to Douglas, but the debates made Lincoln famous. Lincoln decided to run for office again. He eventually won and his efforts freed many slaves.

Robert E. Lee was one of the South's best leaders. Robert E. Lee defeated two Union attacks on Richmond, Virginia. Lee used all of his skills to fight off Grant's army. Robert E. Lee fought in the Mexican War. He was respected in the South. Robert E. Lee was a good leader, but he did not lead the South to victory.

Ulysses S. Grant was the Union military leader. General Grant fought in the Mexican War just like Robert E. Lee. Grant planned to lead an army into Virginia. Ulysses S. Grant became famous for his determination to win. Grant also ordered General William Sherman to lead the Union army into Tennessee. Ulysses S. Grant helped the Union win the war.

The Civil War was very hard for the Union soldiers. Abraham Lincoln freed the slaves to help the Union. Robert E. Lee failed to lead the South to victory. Ulysses S. Grant led the Union into the Civil War. America was forever changed.

Water
Nick C.
Ms. French, 5th Grade

Do you like to drink water? If you don't drink one or two cups of water a day your health is in danger. Did you know you don't need food to live? You only need water to live. Unfortunately water is a valuable resource most of us don't treasure. Water is one of the most used and needed resources in the world. Over 2/3 of the world is covered with water. When the news says there is a drought and some people freak out, they have a reason because that special resource is running out. Do you leave the sink on when you brush your teeth? If you do you are wasting a lot of water. There are countries that don't have as much water as the United States. Did you know that there is a big whirlpool of trash out in the middle of the Pacific Ocean? Most animals in the ecosystem die from this big, monstrous whirlpool. When people dispose of their trash in the ocean the animals find it and eat it. Most people that study the ecosystem find these dead animals with the trash in their stomachs.

Water is also very helpful for plants too. Plants need water to grow. There are a lot of people trying to persuade us to help take care of our water. Most people don't care about our water and say the water will be there. Why take care of it? If you don't take care of it, it won't be there.

Water is our most important natural resource. Always take care of the water. Don't pollute it selfishly. Help the community by cleaning lakes and ponds. Don't waste water at home. We can make a difference.

Barack Obama
Kaylee M.
Ms. Carmack, 4th Grade SAGE

What do I think it means to be a genius? I think it means that you don't give up easily and are smart about one subject. I feel that Barack Obama is a genius because he has to talk in front of millions and work out many different problems. My person's intelligence is interpersonal. The reason I think he is interpersonal because he has to be able to talk to many people.

Barack Obama was born on August 4, 1961. In 1971 Barack Obama moved to Hawaii to go to school and live with his grandparents. His grandfather had served in Patton's army.

Barack's father whom he was named after, died in 1995 of a bad car accident.

After graduating high school he attended College in Los Angeles, California. He graduated with a degree in political science from Columbia University in 1983. Obama enrolled in Harvard Law School in Cambridge, Massachusetts. in1988. He was elected the first African American president of the Harvard Law Review.

Obama moved back to Chicago, got married and entered politics. In 2004 was elected to the US Senate. In November of 2008 he was elected President of the United States. His presidential inauguration was on January 20, 2009. He is really pushing for health care reform because he believes that everyone should have health care. He is also doing everything to try to make this economy better in these days. Obama has a wife and her name is Michelle Obama. He also has two daughters. One is named Malia and she is 10 years old. The other is named Sasha and she is 7 years old.

The wonderful personality traits that Obama has is that he is understanding, loyal, kind, and most of all he is a good leader. I think he is the best president we have ever had. His father and mother have always supported him in whatever choice that he has made. Some lessons that you can learn from him are his story is America and never feel bad if someone tells you that something you said is not true.

Nick Jonas
Brady W.
Ms. Carmack, 4th Grade SAGE

A genius is a person who is very intelligent and always tries their best to figure out something no matter what. I think Nick Jonas is a genius because he is able to write songs and he has to match up all of the music for his group to sing. Nick's dominant intelligence is intrapersonal because he sits in his room most of the time all by himself. It's all worth it though because by the time he comes out of his room he has a new hit single!

Nick Jonas was born in Dallas, Texas on September 16th, 1992. His birth name is Nicholas Jerry Jonas. His common nickname is Nick J. Nick's height is 5'9". Some of his trademarks are his luscious, spontaneous, curly brown hair! One other trademark Nick has is his cute dark brown eyes. Most people think that the Jonas Brothers grew up in Dallas, Texas, but they didn't! I don't know about the rest of Nick's family, but Nick was *born* in Dallas, Texas and grew up in Wyckoff, New Jersey and now resides in Los Angeles with his family. Speaking of Nick's family, he has 3 brothers, 1 mom, and 1 dad. His mom's name is Denise and is a stay at home mom. His dad's name is Paul and he works with Nick and his brothers.

Nick Jonas was discovered while getting his hair cut! His barber was always mentioning that he could sing, so after that, Nick took off in his solo career. The next time Nick got his haircut was about 5 months later, but this time Joe, Kevin, and Frankie came with them. What the barber, Nick's mom and dad and Frankie didn't know was that Joe, Kevin and Nick had been trying to write a song all night and they had succeeded! So, right after Nick was done he started to sing a little bit, then Joe and Kevin started to back him up! Right then their dad knew that he had to do something about this wonderful talent that 3 out of 4 of his sons had!

About 7 months of searching for a song writer, a music director, a choreographer and an agent, they finally found all of them! So then they started to write music and record their music videos. Nick's career has set off wonderfully from my perspective! He has accomplished about everything that he said that he was going to do when he was a little kid. Nick and his family have about 12 concerts a week! Nick plays the electric and acoustic guitar, piano, and the drums! He absolutely loves and enjoys playing all of these instruments.

Sadly Nick was diagnosed with Type 1 diabetes in 2005, while on one of his tours with his two brothers Joe and Kevin. To treat his diabetes he uses The Bayer Contour Meter. Nick says it doesn't hurt, but Joe and Kevin think that it's very painful. Nick has over 456 websites, trying to help parents and kids with any type of diabetes and to help them get through it. He says that he wants the other kids who have diabetes to feel as loved as he does.

Here are some of Nick's fun facts. Nick's favorite baseball team is the New York Yankees. Obviously, his favorite sport is baseball. His favorite player on the Yankees is Derek Jeter and so is mine. Joe says that Nick has almost 200 legendary baseball cards! His favorite football team is the Dallas Cowboys. Nick says that he doesn't tell anybody from outside of his house because they think they will make fun of him. Two of his favorite actors are Matt Long and Keri Lynn Pratt, from the movie *Jack & Bobby*. Nick's favorite movie is *Juno* (2007). His favorite song is *Superstitious* by Stevie wonder. Nick says he doesn't love school, but he doesn't mind it. His favorite subject is geology. His favorite thing to do in school is spell and that is also my favorite thing to do. The Jonas family absolutely loves holidays, every single one! Nick's absolute favorite holiday is Thanksgiving. Nick, Joe, and Kevin all love birthday parties! For Nick's 16th birthday, he received a Pomeranian, and he named it Coco. Now, Nick currently has a Chihuahua named Elvis. Nick Jonas was influenced by his Great Aunt Hilda because he always wanted to be a singer like his aunt.

That's how the Jonas brothers began their careers as pop singing superstars! Here's one of Nick Jonas's favorite personal quotes; "Live like you're on the bottom, even if you know you're on the top." There are a few things some children like me can learn from the things that Nick Jonas does. The most important to me are: never give up, always try your best, and do not ever let someone control your soul of music.

Judy Blume
Tess H.
Ms. Carmack, 5th Grade SAGE

To be a genius you have to be smart, humble, and be able to accept honest criticism. You can NEVER give up. I think that Ms. Blume is a genius because she's able to look at everyone's point of view and she loves drafting and editing her books. She never gives up. Now, Judy is not just a genius she's a linguistic genius (That means she's *'word smart'*, like ME!). I think this is her dominant intelligence because she is funny, good at grammar, and just LOVES to have anything to do with reading. I think many people can learn from Judy because she doesn't stay in a deep, dark depression when her books are rejected or censored. She says "Alright well, let's fix it!" This is a great thing many people do not have. In fact because of her great work and life story, I too, have decided to become an author.

Judy Blume is an author for adult and children's books. She spent her childhood in Elizabeth, New Jersey, making up stories in her head. She says this is what inspired her to write. Only now does she write them on paper. She says that she never once thought of being an author but did think of becoming a detective, cowgirl, a famous actress, or a ballerina. Many adults and children recognize her work. Here are some of her books you may know: <u>Are you there, God: It's Me Margaret</u>, the <u>Fudge</u> reading series,<u> Freckle Juice</u>, <u>Blubber</u>, and <u>Sally J. Freedman Starring as Herself</u>.

Judy is VERY smart! She received a Bachelor's of Science in Education degree from New York University in 1961. The University named her a Distinguished Alumna in 1996. This was the same year the American Library Association honored her with the Margaret A. Edwards Award for Lifetime Achievement. Other recognitions include the Library of Congress Living Legends Award, the 2004 National Book Foundation's Medal for Distinguished Contribution to American Letters, and the University of Southern Mississippi's Medallion for her lifelong contributions to the field of children's literature in 2009. She has written over 21 books that have sold over 80 million copies. All of her young adult novels have been Time Magazine Best Sellers.

Judy believes in sharing her knowledge and helping other authors. She is the founder and trustee of The Kids Fund, a charitable and educational foundation. Ms. Blume serves on 4 different literary boards: The Author's Guild, The Society of Children's Book Writers and Illustrators, The Key West Literary Seminar, and The National Coalition Against Censorship. Other people can learn from her expertise through her service on these boards.

Judy believes that everyone has the right to read what they want. One of her books was at the center of an organized book banning campaign in the 1980's. When she realized this; she began to reach out to other writers, as well as teachers and librarians, who were under fire. As I was looking at her quotes, this one spoke to me, "When I began to write 30 years ago, I didn't know if anyone would publish them. I was lucky. I found a publisher and an editor that was willing to take a chance. They encouraged me. I was never told what I could and could not write. I felt only that I had to write the most honest books I could. It never occurred to me that what I was writing was controversial. Most of it was my feelings and concerns I had when I was young." Since then, she has worked tirelessly with the National Coalition against Censorship to protect the freedom to read. She is the editor of *Places I Never Meant To Be, Original Stories by Censored Writers.*

Most recently, Ms. Blume has completed a four book series -- The Pain & the Great One books -- for young readers. The series was illustrated by *New Yorker* cartoonist James Stevenson, and she has begun work on a new young adult novel. ALL of Judy's work has been translated into 31 languages.

Ms. Blume divorced twice and remarried to George Cooper, a non-fiction writer. He likes to joke:" Hey you get to have all the fun!" She now lives with him on an island on the east coast. They have 3 grown children and 1 grandchild. She also enjoys movies, theater, reading, dancing, New York Mets baseball, and needlepoint. She is 60 years old.

Usain Bolt
Jordan W.
Ms. Carmack, 5th Grade SAGE

I think a genius is someone that works there hardest and doesn't give up. I believe Usain Bolt is a genius because he is the fastest runner in the world and, even though he had some injuries, he never gave up and is consistently practicing his running. Usain Bolt's dominant intelligence is bodily-kinesthetic because he is the fastest person in world, and is awesome in track and field.

Usain Bolt was born August 21, 1986 to his mother, Jennifer, and his dad, Wellesley Bolt, in Trelawney, Jamaica. Usain Bolt's childhood dream was to play cricket and football. He went to Waidensia Primary and All Age School, and then to William Kibb High School. When he went to Waidensia, he was awarded the fastest runner of the 100 meter race. When he was in high school his cricket coach suggested that he should try track. Because he was so fast Bolt won his first silver medal ever in the 200 meter race with a time of 22.04 seconds.

When Usain Bolt was 15, he won one gold and two silver medals in the 2002 World Junior Championships in Kingston. When Usain Bolt was 15, he suffered a series of injuries, but recovered and still runs. Usain Bolt became a professional in 2004 with a new coach, Fitz Coleman. In the same year Usain Bolt had a hamstring and leg injury. In 2005 Usain Bolt had a new coach, Glen Mills. Usain Bolt reached the top 5 runners in the world in 2005-2006. Usain Bolt can't be stopped! He won lots of other awards around the world in track and field.

Usain Bolt became really well known across the world at the 2008 Olympics in Beijing , china by breaking 3 world records and received three gold medals. First he blew through the 100 meter in 9.69 seconds easily. Then he dominated the 200 meter, and broke Mike Johnson's 12-year old recorded. Finally Bolt ran the third leg of Jamaica's 4+100 meter relay, and helped Jamaica easily win the gold in that event also. Usain Bolt, world's fastest man, may go for four gold medals at the 2012 Olympics in London.

Usain was given a new BMW (a nice sports car) from Puma after his great performance in the 2008 Olympics. He had never driven before, so he went to school to learn how to drive his BMW. He ended up in a car crash and totaled the car, but luckily he walked away with only scratches. After the accident, he went to Spanish town, near Kingston where he was treated before he went home. I hope he is much more careful if he decides to try his hand at driving again! Maybe he should stick with running.

Usain Bolt never gave up even when he lost or even when he had injuries and he had confidence. Bolt was so remarkable because he was so fast. Jesse Owens influenced Bolt. Bolt had great achievements. Bolt never gives up and he always follows his dream till he completes them.

Martin Luther King Jr.
Chase E.
Ms. Carmack, 5th Grade SAGE

A genius is person who is a critical thinker and must have patience. Martin Luther King Jr. is a genius because he had to make up many speeches and think them through. His dominant intelligence was interpersonal because he was a people person.

Martin Luther King Jr. was alive from 1929 to 1968. He had a dream that someday blacks would not be treated any different than whites. He also was an interpersonal intelligence learner, just like me. What is an interpersonal learner you ask? Well it is a people person basically. That is probably why he wasn't afraid to stand up to millions of people who were against him.

Sadly he was assassinated in 1968, in Memphis, Tennessee. He had been a pastor in Montgomery, Alabama. He wanted to be free and have peace. He won a Nobel Peace Prize in 1964. He was a very brave man. At one point firemen were hosing down blacks in the street. It was a very bad time.

Even as a child Martin did not agree with segregation. He and his siblings took piano lessons from their mother. They liked to play sports too. Martin was a paper boy. He wanted to be a fireman. He went to elementary school when he was five but could not continue until he was six (he also went to high school). Christine and Alfred were his siblings. And that is Martin Luther King Jr's childhood.

Henry David Thoreau's writing from the 1800's influenced King. Some of his writings were: Smoke, The Moon, and Prayer. Martin had a wife and four children. His wife's name was Coretta

Scott King. King's first child was born in 1955. In 1956 King's house was bombed.

King was involved with many other acts against segregation. For instance, the bus boycott began because Rosa Parks had gotten on the bus. She was tired and blacks were only allowed to sit in the back of the bus. But Rosa Parks sat in the front, no matter who told her to move or any other excuse. To tell you how bad secretion was blacks and whites had separate water fountains and bathrooms. Martin was against all of these crazy laws. Martin Luther King Jr. had an effect on many people's lives today and tomorrow. Martin Luther King Jr. was a big leader in anti-segregation.

Martin only wanted peace, one of his famous quotes was, "Darkness cannot drive out darkness; only light can do that; Hate cannot drive out hate; only love can do that". The point is that we are all the same on the inside and that is just what Martin was trying to say. His name is still not forgotten today.

King was admirable man. He could have taught you a lot of things but let's look up to him by never giving up, staying strong, and believing in yourself…. let's be a… KING!

Helen Keller
Reanna W.
Ms. Carmack, 5th Grade SAGE

A genius is someone who is very intelligent and smart. A genius is someone who will never give up on something the first time. Helen Keller was an intrapersonal genius because even though she could not see or hear, she still wrote a book and learned how to live a very successful life. Although she was blind and deaf, that did not stop her from a living great life. Helen Keller was a very deep thinker and a great author.

Helen Keller was born on June 27th 1880 in Tuscumbia, Alabama. She lived in a house built by her grandparent in 1829. She was born being able to hear and see. But when she was 19 months old she became very sick with a fever. The doctor said that having such a high fever, called brain fever, caused her to be deaf and blind. Helen Keller was so ill some people thought she would die. The first years of her life with this disability were very hard for her. She was very destructive and angry and couldn't understand the world she lived in. Some of her family members requested she be put in an institution.

A family friend named Alexander Graham Bell, who also invented the telephone, felt so badly for her he wanted to try to help. He sent a close friend named Anne Sullivan, a graduate of Perkins School for the Blind, to try to help. Anne was the perfect person for Helen because she had been blind also until she had several surgeries to correct her vision. Anne was able to teach Helen to read in raised print. During their time together, Helen started acting normal and not so angry.

Helen Keller learned so much over the years with her teacher Anne Sullivan she was able to go to college. In 1898 she went to Cambridge School for Girls and later was ready to go to Radcliffe College. She graduated from Radcliffe in 1900 with a Bachelor Degree of Arts. Through the years she continued her studies and had a lot of honors from many people. She received honorary doctoral degrees from Temple University and Harvard University and from the Universities of Glasgow, Scotland; Berlin, Germany; Delhi, India; and Witwatersrand in Johannesburg, South Africa. She was also an Honorary Fellow of the Educational Institute of Scotland.

Even though she was blind and deaf she inspired many people. She started writing off and on over a 50 year period and finally published a book called The Story of My Life. It was an autobiography of all of the many great things she had done including being in the Hall of Fame for Leaders and Legends for the Blindness Field. She also started many foundations to help other blind and deaf people.

Helen stopped making public appearances in 1961. She spent the rest of her years spending time with friends and family. She continued to read. Some of her favorite things to read were the Bible, poetry and philosophy. Helen Keller lived from 1880-1968. She died June 1st, 1968. She was 88 years old when she died.

Helen was influenced by the story of a deaf and blind girl in Norway. Her name was Ragnhild Kata and she gave Helen the idea to get a speaking teacher. Anne Sullivan was very influential in her life because she was the teacher who worked with Helen and taught her how to speak. There are a lot of important life lessons any young person might learn from the way Helen Keller lived. Helen did not give up when she was blind or deaf. She was hopeful that if she got a speaking teacher she would speak. Helen Keller was a great person. She was strong and someone who never gave up.

Leonardo Da Vinci
Griffin L.
Ms. Carmack, 5th Grade SAGE

I think to be a genius you need to see the world differently in your own way. I believe Leonardo Da Vinci was a genius because of his beautiful artwork and genius inventions. Da Vinci's dominant intelligence was logical mathematical because of his scientific discoveries and inventions.

Da Vinci was a man far ahead of his time. I'm going to tell you the story of his life. Da Vinci was born in Vinci, 1452 and lived with his mother. This would make life harder in the future. He received basic education in Math, Language Arts, Reading and Writing. But he became interested in science from his uncle teaching it to him. When he was fifteen his parents put him under the guidance of artist Andrea Del Verrocchio. He owned a famous workshop in Florence. Da Vinci was trained in painting, sculpting, construction and engineering.

In 1482 Da Vinci worked for The Duke of Milan. He made paintings and inventions for the duke. He stayed in Milan until 1499. These were his most artistic years. He made six masterpieces while in Milan. Da Vinci made numerous amounts of inventions in Milan too. Da Vinci had a very scientific side and his notebooks showed it. He showed how birds flew in his notebooks. This gave him ideas of inventing planes and helicopters. So he invented a glider that worked. He drew countless observations and inventions in his notebooks. Da Vinci drew what the body looked like in and out by depicting corpses. This led to him discovering many ways to cure sickness and injuries. He wrote all his studies in his notebooks thoughout his life.

In 1503 Da Vinci went back to Florence. Mainly he worked on his scientific studies. But he made a few more paintings. Everyone did not like these paintings since they liked The Last Supper so much better because it was a religious painting of Jesus during a religious period. Da Vinci also studied how birds fly and how the body works while in Florence.

In 1516 Da Vinci worked for a young French king named Francis1. Da Vinci made one more painting before passing away. Da Vinci died in 1519 he was buried in a church in Italy. Everyone knew his name before he died because of his inventions, paintings, and sculptures. He was a man far ahead of his time.

I've learned many things from Da Vinci. One is if you're

kind, people will trust you with a lot of things. Also, it does not matter where you come from. Another one is you should believe in yourself. These are the things I've learned from Da Vinci.

Ulysses S. Grant
Nacirema U.
Ms. Carmack, 5th Grade SAGE

If you ask me, to be a genius you have to not really know that you're a genius and you mostly are a genius at just one main thing and you're really good at it. You look at the world differently and you won't stop until you figure something out. Sometimes you have to work to be a genius or sometimes you're just born that way. Ulysses S. Grant was a genius because he never gave up and kept on going. He was very good at strategizing plans and other things and that's why he was a major general. I think Grant's dominant intelligence was Interpersonal because while he was the president he gave a lot of speeches to the USA. As general he had to tell all his army men what to do and he was a great leader. I don't think I could be as brave as Ulysses S. Grant in giving orders to people that disliked him.

Ulysses S. Grant was born in Pleasant Point, Ohio on April 27, 1822. Ulysses S. Grant was named Hiram Ulysses when he was born but adopted his other name in the army. He graduated in 1843. Grant then served in the Mexican War. Grant once said of the Mexican war, "One of the most unjust ever waged on a weaker country by a one." I like that motto!

After the war Grant married a woman named Juliet Dent who owned a rich plantation. Grant was chosen to a great task in the United States and had to go to the North West Pacific and leave his family behind. If that was me I would be very sad! In 1854 he resigned from the military because he got caught drinking in his cabin and they did not allow that. He had an addiction to alcohol. I hope that he stopped!!!

After resigning from the military, he went to the east to start other businesses but each one he tried, failed. In April of 1861 he went to his brother and worked at his leather shop in Illinois. Even though he resigned from his military position in West Point, he was not able to find a position in Union General George B. McClellan's staff. His first position in the Civil War was as Colonel of the 'Governor Gate." After doing well with that, he was promoted to Brigadier General on August 7th, 1861.

Being so good he received a big promotion as permanent Major General. I love that he is succeeded so much after all those hard trials!

In April 1862, Grant and his army moved to Shiloh, Tennessee (that's probably the worst thing he ever did besides going for president!!) On their first day of war they were almost defeated and some of the soldiers were badly wounded and some were even killed! As they say in those times "mortally wounded" but I don't know why they just can't say they were killed! It's very strange. Thanks to General Don Buell they turned it over on the second day by getting some of his troops and fought back! He soon took order of many other troops. Abe Lincoln liked Grant so much he changed him to Lieutenant General of all Northern Armies. GO GRANT! Finally the war ended when General Lee surrendered to Grant. After the war Grant was promoted to General in Chief and served just for a while as Secretary Of War under Andrew Johnson.

Since Grant was so popular he won as President of the United States on the Republican side. During Grant's presidential years, he was known as a very honest man even though he did not make good decisions as a president. The bad decisions made him look like a bad president. He was not very good with political things as he was a good general and soldier. When he was President there were problems about race and a lot of scandal. After he served his 2 terms, he went bankrupt from an investment!!! Poor Grant!!! After years of smoking cigars, Grant was stricken with throat cancer, and during this time, he wrote the Personal Memoirs of U.S. Grant, which earned his family $450,000. That was good they got that money after being bankrupt. The Memoirs became an American classic. Grant died at Mount McGregor, New York on July 23, 1885.

Ulysses S. Grant's life was remarkable because he went from a failing soldier to a General to The President of the United States! That's like going from a prey to predator. The influential person that helped make Grant who he was Honest Abe. Lincoln believed in Grant so much that he appointed Grant the general for the Northern Armies. What made Grant want to become a President is the people. The lessons that I learned from Grant is to never give up and that even if you fail at one thing it does not mean you will fail at another thing.

Galileo Galilee
Jack N.
Ms. Carmack, 5th Grade SAGE

I think to be a genius you need to connect to more things than others. You need to be able link to all kinds of things instead of just one thing. I think Galileo Galilee was a genius because he proved that the earth revolved around the sun and he made one of the first telescopes. I think Galileo's dominant intelligence is Logical Mathematical because he had to know angles to prove the earth and other planets revolved around the sun.

Galileo was born in Italy in 1564. Galileo was the first child. Galileo moved probably five times before he turned 10. In 1575 Galileo turned 11 and he was sent to school to study language, math, religion, music, and art. Galileo's father sent him to Florence to study with the monks. When he was 17, he was sent to medical school. Galileo's father, Vicenzo, was a musician. Vicenzo died at the age of 78. Galileo's mother's name was Guilia. Galileo's mother decided to build their home in the countryside of Pisa. Galileo lived with Muzio Tedald, after his father died.

While Galileo was at church he noticed a lamp swinging back and forth but there was no draft and he wanted to find out why. Then when he was exploring possible solutions he decided to try an experiment. He found out about the laws of the pendulum. Galileo had just found out the world is not flat it's round! Then Galileo came up with the idea of a pendulum clock. Galileo wanted to tell the world what he just found out so he wrote a book. Oh, and he got sent to jail for going against the religious beliefs, but his theory was correct.

I think the character traits that helped Galileo were his love for math and his adventurous attitude. I think his life was remarkable because he did what he wanted when he wanted. I don't think there were any people that influenced him because his father wanted him to be a doctor and his sisters and mother didn't think much about what he did. Galileo seemed to be a person who was very intrinsically motivated. I learned that you should always do what you believe in and never do something because someone told you to.

Bruce Lee
Ethan G.
Ms. Carmack, 5th Grade SAGE

I think in order to be a genius you have to be talented or good at something. I feel that Bruce Lee was a bodily – kinesthetic genius because he was a great martial artist and he was good at acting and created his own form of martial arts.

Bruce Lee was born on November 27, 1940. He was also raised in three different locations known as San Francisco, California, Hong Kong and Seattle, Washington. The story of Bruce's birth is that his dad was a performer who was working in America and had brought his wife with him. At the time, Bruce's mother was pregnant and Bruce was born in America. Bruce's childhood probably wasn't the best because his parents had a fear of demons stealing young boys so they dressed him up as a girl and sent him to a girl school.

When Bruce was a teenager he was involved in both gang activity and dance. In dancing he won a cha cha championship and in gang activity he risked his life out on the streets. Bruce started to study kung fu in case he got in a fight without his gang. When Bruce was in high school he was very good at acting and he was offered a lot of money, but Bruce had to leave for America because he got in trouble for fighting. Bruce did the rest of high school in Washington. When he graduated he was a martial arts teacher and created his own form of martial arts known as Jeet kune do and married a woman named Linda Emery.

In Hong Kong Bruce created a movie known to the U.S.A. as Fists of Fury which was released in 1971. Soon Bruce created his own movie company known as Concord Pictures. Sadly, Bruce never lived to become very famous and died on July 20, 1973. At first they said his death was caused by an aspirin that made his brain swell. Some people have other theories like poison, hit man, and curses. His death is kind of a mystery but it's most likely to be the aspirin that killed him.

The personalities and traits that made Bruce who he was is that he set lots of goals, took plenty of chances, and never ever gave up. Some of the people who influenced him were Yip man, who was his martial arts teacher and Taky Kimura, who was his student, friend, and business partner. Some lessons that can be learned from him are if you never give up, you will be successful.

Lance Armstrong
Connor S.
Ms. Carmack, 5ᵗʰ Grade SAGE

There are many types of geniuses. A genius is a person that never gives up and works hard to meet their goals. Lance Armstrong is a genius because he is a very good biker and overcame cancer. He also does many things that impress me. Lance's dominant intelligence is bodily-kinesthic because he is very athletic and is very good at what he does.

Lance had a very poor mom. She was a secretary and worked overtime to get more money. His mom got the money for a bike when he was seven. Lance rode everyday on his bike. When he crashed he would always get right back on. He would ride ten miles in the morning, then ride to school, and when he got home he would ride another ten miles. Lance would also ride his bike to Oklahoma and he would have to call his mom to get him. Armstrong liked running so he would run six miles after school. He tried other sports like football, soccer, tennis, and basketball but didn't like them very much. Armstrong was a very intelligent, athletic, and smart kid.

Armstrong participated in triathlons where you bike, run, and swim at the age of 13. Lance was trying to become a professional cyclist. Lance raced in Junior Championships and came in first many times. I think he got his dream because he was making $20,000 per year by the time he was 17. He was so involved in biking that he didn't graduate on time like he should have. His mom made him take private lessons. Armstrong still impressed me when he was a teenager.

Lance had a great professional life and is still having one. He is one of a few in millions that have survived testicular cancer. After Lance overcame cancer he opened a foundation called Live Strong. Live Strong is a foundation/charity that tries to find a cure for cancer. Lance also won Tour de France seven times in a row. Armstrong has won many other races too.

Armstrong is so determined, hard working and smart to do whatever he wants. His mom has encouraged him from learning how to ride a bike to winning Tour de France. Armstrong has researched many bikes to find the right one. He is remarkable because he overcame cancer, he stayed with it even through the tragic times, he is one of the best bikers in the world, and has won many races. I hope you have learned a lot so you can become a biker, singer, astronaut or whatever you want to be just never give up and chase your dreams.

John Lennon
Blake F.
Ms. Carmack, 5th Grade SAGE

I believe that to be a genius, you have to be very smart in one particular area and never give up when things get hard. I think that John Lennon's dominant intelligence is musical because he was in the most famous rock band all time. Many musicians today credit John Lennon and the Beatles as their musical inspiration.

On October 9th, 1940 John Lennon was born into a normal working family in Liverpool, England. His parents separated when he was young and John was raised by his aunt "Mimi". When he was five, his mom, Julia, gave him his first guitar. John's constant playing prompts brought his aunt to say, "The guitar's all very well as a hobby, John, but you'll never make a living out of it." She was wrong.

In 1956, when John was in high school, he met bassist Paul McCartney and they formed their first rock band, The Quarrymen. Then one year later Paul introduced George Harrison to their band at a basement club called the Morgue. Two years later, their band's name changed to The Beatles and they made their first debut in Hamburg, West Germany, with Stu Sutcliff on bass and Pete Best on the drums. In 1960, Brian Epstein, a local record store owner, introduced The Beatles to the world, and this is how John Lennon became famous. In 1964 The Beatles began their first U.S. tour at the Coliseum in Washington, D.C.

John Lennon was always honest and outspoken. John Lennon changed people's perspectives about war and other people. Many government officials thought he was dangerous, but he was very nonviolent and just wanted world peace. During the early 1970's he fought the U.S. government to avoid deportation. Unfortunately, a brilliant life came to an untimely end on December 8th 1980. John was heading home from a recording session when he was shot by John Bohannan and Stephanie Shelton.

John was very obsessive about his music never gave up and didn't care what anyone thought about it. Even though he was dyslexic he always stayed true to himself and never gave up. The people that were most important to him were Brian Epstein, because he introduced the Beatles, The Beatles, because they were his closest friends and the ones he made music with, Yoko Ono, because she was his wife, and Julia and Alfred Lennon, because they were his parents, so, John really did always get by with a little help from his friends.

Annie Leibovitz
Rebekah O.
Ms. Carmack, 5th Grade SAGE

What do you think it means to be a genius? I think a genius is someone who sticks to their goal and is very intelligent with what they do. I think Annie Leibovitz is a genius because you have to know many things to be a photographer. You also have to be very focused to do something like Annie. I think Annie's dominant intelligence is Spatial because she is very creative.

Annie Leibovitz [real name Anna-lou] was born in 1949 in Waterbury, Connecticut. Her father worked in the Air Force. She started working for *Rolling Stone* magazine in 1970. Her first cover story was for John Lennon. She became chief photographer in 1976. Annie worked for *Rolling Stone* for ten years and made one hundred forty two photos, stories, and essays. After she quit her job for *Rolling Stone* she joined the staff for Vanity Fair in 1983. Annie writes many books about her childhood. Annie was #1 for the photo of John Lennon the day he was shot. Annie lives in New York with her three children, Sarah, Susan, and Samulle.

Annie Leibovitz received numerous awards for her excellent photographs. She is going to receive an award from the Georgia O'Keeffe museum for 2010 Women of Distinction because Leibovitz has been the best photo journalist for forty years and has made many memorable portraits for museums. Annie was part of Barnard College medal distinction. She has won many other awards such as: "Living Legend" in 2000 and was one of 35 "Inventors of Our Time" by *Smithsonian Magazine* in 2005. People say that Leibovitz has made more photographs than any other photographer in the world in one year.

Some of Annie's personality traits helped her achieve. Today Annie is one of the world's most famous photographers. How did she become so famous? Leibovitz has to be able to work with anybody. I think she is so remarkable because she gets so many calls from famous people from all over the world because she is so well known. Some of them she has never even heard of.

Annie was inspired by her mother. Her mother used to take so many pictures that she had to buy Annie her own [fake] camera since she did everything her mom did. Annie became a photographer because she loved taking pictures. Three things that I or another person could learn from Annie are that if you set your mind to something, you can do it. I also learned to stick to what you know and what you like and finally don't quit.

Vincent Van Gogh
Isabella W.
Ms. Carmack, 5th Grade SAGE

Vincent Van Gogh was a genius because he was creative and educated. He was a genius because he was a talented artist and never gave up. I feel that Van Gogh's intelligence was dominant spacial because he loved painting and drawing and was an amazing artist.

Vincent Van Gogh was born in Groot-Zundurt, Holland on March 10, 1853. His father was the preacher of a protestant church. Van Gogh had severe mental problems for most of his life. He had three sisters and two brothers. One of his brothers, Theo, was his closest and best friend.

Van Gogh moved to Paris in 1886 and went to live with his brother, Theo. He was inspired by various artists to lighten his paints and experiment painting with a broken brush. He also tried small strokes of pure color used by the Neo-Impressionists. Vincent loved living with his brother Theo.

In February 1888 he left Paris and went to live in Arles, where he hoped to set up a community of artists. He was captivated by the vibrant colors of the spring landscape. He also tried small strokes of pure color used by the neo-impressionists. Van Gogh produced 14 paintings in less than one month and varied his painting techniques. The painter Paul Gauguin joined him in October of 1888. Gauguin left Van Gogh two months later, bringing him to cut off part of his left ear with a razor. He was then taken to the hospital and released in January of 1889 only to suffer another mental setback which returned him to the hospital in February of 1889.

Afraid of having another breakdown, Vincent voluntarily moved to the asylum at Saint-Remy, May 1889. Over the next year he made 150 paintings and some amazing drawings. He then went Auvers-sur-Oise, where he was under the care of Dr. Paul Gachet, a physician and amateur painter. Over just two months Van Gogh made a painting each day. On July 27, 1890, he attempted suicide in a wheat field, shooting himself in the chest, and then died two days later from the wound.

Vincent Van Gogh was very lonely and dark which inspired him to draw his amazing, sad drawings. His life was remarkable because he drew so many drawings and never gave up. His biggest inspiration was his brother, Theo, who was an art dealer who also took care of Vincent. We can learn from him to never give up. One thing we could learn not to do is to never drink or do drugs. Even though Van Gogh did many wrong things he was still an amazing artist and spatial genius.

Pablo Picasso
Katie M.
Ms. Carmack, 4th Grade SAGE

To be a genius you have to be very bright in your dominant intelligence and never give up. People will look up to you. I think Pablo is a genius because he is very smart when it comes to painting and sculpting. I think his dominant intelligence is spatial because he painted and sculpted and was a very good modern artist.

Pablo started painting when he was very little. He was born in 1881. In 1895, his dad, Don José, got a professorship at La Lonja, the school of fine arts in Barcelona, Spain. The family settled there. Pablo passed the entrance in an examination in an advanced course in classical art and still life at the same school. Pablo was better than the senior students doing the final exam projects they had from the moment he began. When his dad saw how good Pablo was, he gave Pablo his palette and paintbrush. Then his dad said he would never himself paint again because Pablo was just naturally so much better than he was.

Picasso created a new kind of art called Cubism. He also created synthetic cubism. Cubism is a type of art created by geometric shapes. It shows pictures from different points of view and angles. They have different strange designs. Pablo's cubism is unusual and crazy. One of his paintings was Tete de Cheval - it was worth millions of dollars! Another one of his painting was The Old Guitarist. It was worth $149,000 dollars! He also made The Tomato Plant. It was worth $129,000 dollars! He was the most famous modern artist of all time.

The personality trait that helped him achieve success was that he enjoyed painting. He also painted certain things according to his feelings. He was very creative. He could paint and create forever- in fact he did until he died. Pablo did what he thought was great art regardless of what others thought.

There were two main people who influenced Pablo to be this amazing artist. They were his dad, Don Josie, and his teacher. Even though he had a lot of controversy in his life, Pablo always appreciated this wonderful thing called art.

Mozart
Nicolette W.
Ms. Carmack, 4ᵗʰ Grade SAGE

To be a genius is to have people to look up to you. Geniuses don't give up very easily. That's what it means to be a genius. Mozart could compose entire symphonies in his head. He could imagine the sounds in his head without hitting a single note. Wow! He composed lots of symphonies in his head. He was a musical genius. He is the most well known classical musical composer.

Mozart was playing the clavichord by the age of three. When he was four, he began writing short compositions. At the age of five, he started writing original works. At the age of six he learned to play the violin without receiving lessons. Mozart was the last of seven children of whom five did not survive early childhood. Only one survived and was four when Mozart was born. Mozart probably died of strep throat. Some say he was poisoned, some say he had kidney failure.

He composed many great symphonies. His work inspired other musicians, and he started to introduce the piano by playing the key board. He became very successful by not giving up and being smart in that specific area. He composed symphonies. He started a musical life at the age of three when he started playing instruments. His musical career started at the age of three going all the way up to the end of his life and he was very famous. His dad, Leopold, was a violinist and composer. He realized when Mozart sat in front of the keyboard that his son was a musical genius, following his steps.

Every piece of music he created was amazing, from the first pieces he composed as a five year old, to the requiem he was working on when he died right before his 35ᵗʰbirthday. Mozart wrote an astonishing amount of beautiful music. Mozart was no doubt the greatest child star that ever lived. He was traveling all over Europe playing music by the time he was six. Because of his constant traveling, he eventually learned fifteen languages. He wrote his first sonata for the piano when he was four and composed his first opera when he was twelve.

When he grew up, Mozart moved to Vienna, and tried to earn a living as a pianist and composer. But he had a bit of trouble hiding that he was no longer a child prodigy. Mozart was still a musical genius, but after he was no longer a cute kid, people stopped making a big fuss about him. Back then, musicians were treated like servants, but Mozart refused to be treated like a servant. Mozart had such genius for combining music and theater that he took opera to a whole new level. No other composer from Mozart`s time has so many operas all over the world.

Mozart wrote 600 works including 41 symphonies and 27 piano concertos. Three of his most famous operas include The Marriage at Figaro, The Magic Flute, and Don Giovvoni. Mozart loved composing music and never stopped as long as he lived. He was always looking at ways to improve his pieces or do something different or more complicated and worked very hard his whole life doing what he loved. He was the most amazing composer that ever lived!

Frank Marshall
Grace G.
Ms. Carmack, 4th Grade SAGE

A genius is someone who is very smart and uses their intelligence to do work and not to show off. I think Frank Marshall was a genius because he was one of the world's strongest chess players in the early part of the twentieth century. He was an English world champion chess player. He was a spatial genius because he knew where to move the pieces before he did it and knew how to beat the person and how they played before he played the match. He knew where all the pieces went because he had been playing for a long time. In fact, he had been playing ever since he was eight years old. He continued to play chess until he was sixty-seven years old.

Frank Marshall was born in New York but grew up in Canada. He lived in Montreal, Canada from 1885-1904. Mr. Marshall once won a championship but did not accept the title because the current championship winner did not compete. Another time the current championship winner died, so Marshall did not accept the award again. He felt like he did not earn it because he did not beat him while he was still living. Marshall played a match against the new World Chess Champion and lost eight games. He learned that he wasn't the best, and that everyone can lose every now and then. He finally became one of the grand masters in 1914. He opened a Marshall Chess Club in 1915. Frank Marshall held the United States Title for twenty nine years straight! He was a great chess player but it was a very demanding lifestyle. I bet sometimes he wished he could have a normal life.

Frank Marshall showed great sportsmanship. One of the

things that made him a good sport is that he gave up some of the U.S. championships when the current championship winners didn't compete. It made him feel like he wasn't the real winner. He was a world famous chess player and a lot of people came to see him play. In one match in 1909, he lost eight games and he drew for fourteen! That match had a major influence on him because he realized that he couldn't win every game.

In conclusion, I learned three lessons from the great chess player Frank Marshall. Number one, it's important to be a good sport. Number two, you can't always win. And number three, if you work hard for something, it just might come true.

Albert Kahn
Ashley B.
Ms. Carmack, 4th Grade SAGE

A genius is someone who has exceptional intellectual ability and originality. A genius is also someone who doesn't give up very easily. I think Albert Kahn was a genius because he had to be very smart to design a fifth of the world's buildings and factories. I think Albert Kahn was dominant spatial intelligence because he was a great architect and builder. He also developed plants to build army tanks during World War II. You need to be creative to make things and to design things.

Albert Kahn was the oldest child out of eight children. He and his family moved to Echternach, Luxembourg near Ruhr Valley a little while after he was born. They stayed there until Albert turned eleven. Albert's father, Joseph was a rabbi. He was a dreamer and he was looking for work. Albert's mother, Rosalie, had a talent for music and drawing. Rosalie passed on her music talent to Albert who became a very good piano player. Rosalie also passed on her drawing skills to Albert. That's probably how Albert wanted to be an architect when he grew up.

Albert was an apprentice in the early 1880s with Detroit Architectural firm John S. Scott and Associates. He was also an apprentice with Mason and Rice. Albert was an errand boy for Mason and Rice. Albert worked his way up to the top. He became Mason's partner. He also became chief draftsman. Mr. Mason liked his concentration and how he studied. Mason would always invite Albert over to talk about architecture while eating dinner. Mason encouraged Albert to make his drafting skills better. When Albert was 22, he won a $500 traveling scholarship so he could study in Europe. Albert became good friends with

Henry Bacon. Bacon was an architect too. Albert gave Henry credit for encouraging him to further his education.

After his studies in Europe, Albert came back to Detroit and working at Mason and Rice. He stayed there for a lot of years before moving elsewhere. Albert worked with his brother Julius, a civil engineer. During the depression, Albert made over 1,000 factories. Some of them, he made for the Soviet Union. By the late 1930s, Albert had over 600 clients and made nearly a fifth of the buildings in the United States! Albert Kahn died on December 8, 1942. Albert Kahn has been called "The Father of the Modern American Factory".

To be successful like Albert Kahn, you would have to study hard, do well in school, know a lot about a certain area, and not give up very easily. Albert Kahn's parents, especially his mother, influenced him when he was growing up. Albert was also influenced by Henry Bacon and Mason Rice. Mason influenced Albert by encouraging him. Mason encouraged Kahn by telling him that he was a very good man and he was very good in the architectural area. Bacon influenced Kahn by encouraging him to further his education. Albert's mom influenced him by passing on her talents to him and always believing in him.

Some lessons you can learn from Albert Kahn is that he never gave up, he worked hard, and he believed he could do anything if he kept trying. He listened very well to his clients and he didn't act like he had to know everything. He gave everyone else a chance to share their ideas. I learned that it's important to listen to everyone's ideas. Albert Kahn was truly a great architect and I enjoyed learning about him.

Abraham Lincoln
Brady W.
Ms. Carmack, 4th Grade SAGE

A genius is someone who doesn't have to be super smart. You still have to be pretty smart though. You actually try stuff, even if it seems hard. You don't just think about doing something and not do it because you're afraid to mess up. I think Abraham Lincoln was a genius because he was our 16th president and you need to be pretty smart to be president. He knew a lot of stuff about politics. He also kept half of the country from leaving the country and starting their own separate country. If not for Abraham Lincoln, Georgia might not be a part of the United States today! I think his dominant intelligence was interpersonal because he was nice and got along well with a lot of people. He helped free the slaves. He was a respected, great political leader and speaker. He wasn't really shy and nervous.

Some major events that happened in his life were that he lived and grew up in a log cabin in a town called Hardin in Kentucky. As a teen, he was known as a hard working, strong, intelligent man who loved to read. When he was 19, he saw slavery in action and didn't like it at all. He thought it wasn't fair.

There is a story that tells about how he got his famous nickname. He had a job as a store clerk and a lady was at the store and forgot her change after paying for her tea. Abe ran ten miles to her house to give it to her, even though it was a very small amount. That's how he got the nickname "Honest Abe".

The next year, when he was 20, he was in the military and it was his job to get the Indians back off of land white settlers had settled on. When he was a military leader, he discovered he was a good leader and commander.

As a politician, Abraham was elected to the Illinois House of Representatives. He served in the House for eight years. He wanted railroads all across America. He made a lot of speeches against slavery. He studied law to become a lawyer. He also helped a lot of people when they had law problems. Abraham Lincoln got married and had four sons.

Abraham Lincoln lost the first time he ran for President of the United States. He ran against Douglas, but lost. He then helped to form the Republican Party. He was the first candidate nominated to run on this new party's ticket and this time he was elected president in 1861. Lincoln was the 16th president. A terrible thing that happened was that his son died in the White House at 11 years of age. This made Abraham and his wife very sad.

Lincoln was President during the Civil War. He thought slavery was evil, so he made it illegal. Then 6 states, including Georgia, said they weren't part of the country and wanted to start their own country which they called The Confederate States of America. But he was able to stop them and keep us all together as the United States of America.

One person that influenced him is a little girl named Grace Bedell. She influenced him by encouraging him to grow a beard. He looked a bit awkward and she thought a beard would make him look better. She knew that if he looked better he would have a better chance of winning the Presidency. A few things people can learn from him are that even if you don't have much and come from a poor background, through hard work, honesty, and dedication you can still become very successful and rich. We can also learn to stand up for what we believe is right, even if it is not a popular view.

Rachael Ray
Summer C.
Ms. Carmack, 4th Grade SAGE

A genius is somebody who is bright and doesn't give up easily. They are very high in their dominant intelligence. They persevere on what they love the most. I think Rachael Ray is a genius because she does very well in cooking. It takes a lot of courage to be a chef like her. She definitely has the personality and qualities of an interpersonal, mathematical genius. Rachael Ray is interpersonal because she is very nice and VERY down to earth. She is logical-mathematical because she has to know a lot of math to be able to cook and measure very well. I think it would be very interesting (and hard) to be a chef.

She learned how to cook by watching her mom, then by working and cooking in her family's many restaurants. The way she learned how to grill was trying it out in one of the family restaurants and nearly grilling her right thumb off when she was about 3 or 4! She uses boxed ingredients and gives special nicknames and abbreviations. She likes to have fun and act goofy when she is cooking.

Oprah Winfrey helped Rachael's career start. Her company, Harpo, produces Rachael Ray's TV show. Oprah liked Rachael Ray's sense of humor and her beautiful personality. She also liked her quick and easy recipes.

The thing that she is most famous for is the Rachael Ray Show. On this show, you can get great recipes daily, watch celebrity interviews, talk with Rachel's buddies, see musical performances, and more. It has about 2.6 million views every day, so is one of the highest viewed daytime shows. The audience sits in a circle around the rotating stage so they can always see the action. The show has won 2 Daytime Emmy Awards for Outstanding Talk Show Entertainment in 2008 and 2009. In 2007 she made about 6 million dollars a year. I'm sure it's more than that now.

There is more to her than just the Rachael Ray Show. She also has 4 shows on Food Network. They are: "30 Minute Meals", "$40 a Day," "Inside Dish", and "Rachael Ray's Tasty Travels". She also has 14 popular cookbooks and her Every Day with Rachael Ray magazine. She is very peppy and she has had no formal training. She loves her dogs so much she even has pet recipes in her magazine because she thinks they deserve yummy food too! She is very silly, nice, and down to earth.

Rachael Ray had a certain personality that helped her become and stay a professional cook. She never gave up on what she really wanted to achieve. She didn't give up easily at all. She is a very hard worker. She is a very bright woman. Her parents taught her everything she knows, and they taught her to be very nice and kind. We could learn by following the way she acts and by being very nice and kind. We could learn from her by never giving up on ourselves and others. Some famous chefs made fun of her because of how easy her recipes and because she acted silly and goofy. She never gave up on what she believed in. And she never gave up on others.

George Washington
Caleb C.
Ms. Carmack, 4th Grade SAGE

I think a genius is someone who can figure things out most people can't. George Washington was one of those people. He was very smart without any formal education. He was naturally smart. He was able to figure out things most people couldn't. One of his dominant intelligences was spatial, just like me! George Washington was dominant spatial intelligence because he was a great surveyor as well as an amazing speaker & political leader. Another thing that showed his spatial ability is that George loved to play chess as a child, just like me! He lived in Virginia and was born on February 22, 1732.

George Washington was a great leader. He was a Second Rate General in the Revolutionary War; he led troops in the French and Indian War, and was Commander- in-Chief in the Continental Army. He was also a Commander of the Virginia Force.

After serving in the Army, he was elected the first President of the United States of America. He served for two four year terms and refused to hold the office for more than eight years because he thought one man shouldn't rule for so long. Washington was awarded the first Congressional Gold Medal. He died in 1799 and the funeral speech was given by Henry Lee. He stated in the speech that of all Americans, President George Washington was, "first in war, first in peace and first in the hearts of his countrymen."

George Washington was a remarkable man because he was an excellent delegator and judge of talent and character. He knew a lot about leading and did not give up easily. He was influenced by the Fairfax Family. Thomas Fairfax hired George as the first surveyor of the newly created Culpeper County, Virginia. This is where he gained invaluable knowledge of the terrain.

By studying the life of George Washington, I learned that in order to be a great leader, you have to be a great listener. I also learned that I need to work hard and give a lot to what is important to me. George Washington was a great American hero and very interesting to study.

Chapter 7
To Our Brave Armed Forces

Dear American Hero
Laura G.
Ms. Vowell, 1st Grade

My name is Laura. I like horses. I go to Rock Spring Elementary. I think you are a hero because you fight for our country every day. I hope you can see your family at Thanksgiving. Do you have children? Is it messy in your house? Thank you for what you do!

Love, Laura

Dear American Hero
Quinton W.
Ms. Vowell, 1st Grade

My name is Quinton. What do you do at work to help people? Do you like saving people? It is cool to help people. You might miss your family.

Love, Quinton

Dear American Hero
Ireland B.
Ms. Vowell, 1st Grade

My name is Ireland. I am from Rock Spring Elementary. What do you do as a soldier? Thank you for saving our country. I think you are a hero because you help us.

Love, Ireland

Dear American Hero
Ethan R.
Ms. Vowell, 1st Grade

My name is Ethan R. My favorite toy is an Xbox. I think that you are cool. Thank you for helping our country stay safe.

From, Ethan

Dear American Hero
Madison N.
Ms. Vowell, 1st Grade

My name is Madison. I am a 1st grader at Rock Spring Elementary. I think that you are a hero because you are saving our country and that is good to save a lot of people. I am sure that you miss your family but you may can go to your family and you can eat Thanksgiving dinner with them. Thank you for saving our country.

Your friend, Madison

Dear American Hero
Parker R.
Ms. Vowell, 1st Grade

My name is Parker. I am fun to play with. Thank you for keeping our country safe. I wish I could help you be safe. I hope you make it home.

Your friend, Parker

Dear American Hero
Ethan H.
Ms. Vowell, 1st Grade

My name is Ethan H. I go to Rock Spring Elementary. I think you miss your friends. Thank you for fighting for everybody.

Your friend, Ethan

Dear American Hero
Cameron B.
Ms. Vowell, 1ˢᵗ Grade

My name is Cameron at Rock Spring Elementary. Are you having fun at work? I have been waiting for Veteran's Day to come.

Love, Cameron

Dear American Hero
Emily D.
Ms. Vowell, 1ˢᵗ Grade

My name is Emily D. I like soldiers. My favorite toy is a Wii. Thank you for keeping our country safe. I am glad you are here. Do you like being a soldier? Do you know my cousin Brandon? What do you do for America?

Love your friend, Emily

Dear American Hero
Jacob K.
Ms. Vowell, 1ˢᵗ Grade

My name is Jacob. You have work. I wanted to be a hero. Do you have work to do? I bet you miss your family.

Love, Jacob

Dear American Hero
Emily F.
Ms Vowell, 1ˢᵗ Grade

My name is Emily. I love to go somewhere with my mom. Her name is Kirsten. I think you are a hero because you keep us safe.

Love, Emily
P.S. Thank you

Dear Soldier
Jessie C.
Ms. Brown, 1st Grade

You are very brave. You are very strong. The soldiers that died I feel sorry for you. You are the best. We all love you. I wish I could help you. My name is Jessie. Do not forget that God is in your heart.

Love, Jessie

Dear Soldier
Jacob M.
Ms. Winsor, 1st Grade

My name is Jacob. I am a student of Rock Spring Elementary School in McDonough, Georgia. I am in Mrs. Winsor's 1st grade class. How are you? We have been studying about soldiers. You are my hero.

Your friend, Jacob

Dear Soldier
Emma B.
Ms. Winsor, 1st Grade

My name is Emma. I am six years old. I am a first grade student at Rock Spring Elementary School in McDonough, Georgia. I learned about soldiers. I know it is hard being away. I hope you get to come home soon. But you are the best at keeping the country safe. You are very brave.

Your friend, Emma

Chapter 8
Poetry

A Sunny Day in the Meadow
Sierra H.
Ms. Murdock, 3rd Grade

One day I was in the meadow,
Dancing with a friendly fellow.
He looked so nice dressed in yellow,
And my long hair in the air,
By the fields there I go.
Shouting out, "Hello, hello!"
Then I look below my chin,
Then I look up again.

Blue
Abigail S.
Ms. Williams, 4th Grade

Blue-the color of the sky
Blue-the color of the ocean
Blue-the color of some flowers
Blue-the color of some birds
Blue-the color of the chairs in my classroom
Blue-the color of my favorite jacket
Blue-the color of my backpack
Blue-the color rain makes me feel
Blue-the color of my father's eyes
Blue is my favorite color.

Kindness
Mallory A, Summer C, Destiny B, Kayley R, Caleb C, CJ S, and Brady W.
Ms. Partain, 4th Grade

Kind words
I will always be considerate
Nice and respectful
Do caring things
Never be mean
Encourage others
Sincere compliments
Share with others

The Poem that I Waited to Write
Blake F.
Ms. Cochran, 5th Grade

I had this short poem to write.
I waited 'til the very last night.
I couldn't think of a word,
And I felt quite absurd.
To be up writing all night.

I think I might write about a sheep
Who drove my grandfather's new Jeep.
Aha! That's it!
He'll drive me into a pit,
And the pit will be supremely deep.

But is that just it?
Will the sheep just sit?
That will depend
On how I make up the end.
Oh well, I'll just finish this bit.

My Special Hero
Ansley R.
Ms. Cochran, 5th Grade

I watch him prepare his uniform every single day
I hate to say goodbue, it hurts in every way
He fights for all of our freedom
But I wonder if he knows how much we miss him
I cannot wait till he comes home
Because we will not feel all alone
I will wrap my arms around him tight
And know he will be with us tonight
I come to school every day
But cannot wait to see my special hero on this upcoming day!
HOORAY!!!

Rock Spring...A Mixed-emotion, True, Meaningful School
Kaitlin C.
Mr. Griffis, 5th Grade

Pain, we had that the first year of Rock Spring.
Joy, we've had it lots of times.
At Rock Spring we have mixed emotions.
Mixed emotions are a good thing, I guess.
It shows we're real.
It shows we can overcome any pain or grief.
It shows that even if we are lucky enough
To get a lot of joy, it will not go to our heads.
Just because we have mixed emotions,
that doesn't mean we're a bad school.
It means we're a great school.
We have true feelings.
We have true, honest students.
We have the best staff.
Most of all, we have meaningful colors.
Blue stands for pain and grief.
Orange stands for joy and happiness.
Rock Spring is a mixed-emotion, true, meaningful school
And, I'm proud to be a student here.

What is Life Without a Purpose?
Morgan C.
Mr. Griffis, 5th Grade

What is life without a purpose? It is like…
What is a painting without an easel?
What is a globe without a stand?
How can you walk without any legs?
How can you touch without any hands?
How can you write without a pencil?
How can you eat without a mouth?
How can you see without your eye's?
How can you dance without any music?
How can you do anything without a purpose?
You need GOALS!

Me
CJ S.
Ms. French, 5th Grade

I am a football-loving brother who loves eating pizza.
I wonder what I'm eating for dinner.
I hear my brother's rat wake me up.
I see my dog every day.
I want to pass the 5th grade.

I am a football-loving, pizza-eating brother.
I pretend to listen to my mom.
I feel stupid during math.
I touch my dog every day.
I worry I'm not going to pass 5th grade.
I cry when I really hurt.

I am a football-loving, pizza-eating brother.
I understand my four-wheeler is ok.
I say hi.
I dream dirt bikes.
I try to pop wheelies.
I hope I don't crash.

I am a football-loving, pizza-eating brother.

I Am
Ashley N.
Ms. French, 5th Grade

I am a dog-loving girl who likes to sleep in.
I wonder if I will get to buy a PSP.
I hear my neighbor's 4-wheelers every day.
I want a black PSP.
I am a dog-loving girl who likes to sleep in.

I pretend me and my dog are in a wrestling match.
I feel awesome when I'm proud of myself.
I touch my dog when he comes near me.
I worry about getting into college.
I cry when someone upsets me.
I am a dog-loving girl who likes to sleep in.

I understand I have changed a lot.
I say I love you to my parents every day.
I dream to meet Nick Jonas.
I try to do my best in everything.
I hope I am the best child ever.
I am a dog-loving girl who likes to sleep in.

The Antonym Story
Cambrey J.
Ms. Hall, 1st Grade

Dog is fat and short.
Cat is skinny and tall.
Dog is hot.
Cat is cold.
Dog is soft.
Cat is hard.
Dog is so sad.
Cat is so happy.
Dog lives on a big hill.
Cat lives on a small hill.

All About Me
Lorena C.
Ms. French, 5th Grade

I am a soccer-loving sister who understands how to roller skate.
I wonder if I'll pass 5th grade.
I hear the bird chirp every morning before I go to school.
I see my dog waiting for me when I come back from school.
I want to win the lottery.

I am a soccer-loving sister who understands how to roller skate.
I pretend I am brushing my teeth when I am supposed to wash
the dishes.
I feel happy when we go to the fair.
I touch my dog on the nose.
I worry about my dog playing near the street.
I cry when I think of my dead dog.

I am a soccer-loving sister who understands how to roller skate.
I say get out of my room.
I dream of having a car.
I try to eat my fruit.
I hope to win the lottery.

I am a soccer-loving sister who understands how to roller skate.

Ghost
Mrs. LaFiosca
RSE Guidance Counselor

There's a big huge ghost
Who hangs out at my house.
He doesn't make a sound,
He's quiet as a mouse.

But his shadow looms large
Upon my wall
And I hear his footprints
Creeping up the hall.

He likes to wait
For all to fall asleep
Before he begins

His nightly creep.

"CREEK!" The floorboards
Call his name
And I shudder in my pj's
Hoping he is tame.

How can I get
This ghost to leave?
What do I have
I can pull from my sleeve?

Perhaps if I sing
In a crooked key
I will hurt his ghost ears
And he'll have to flee.

Or maybe I can whistle
A scary tune
Of goblins and witches
And places they loom.

Oh! THOSE things won't scare him
How could I forget?
They hang out together
In a shiny Corvette.

I guess I'll give up
And go back to sleep
And dream sweet dreams
Of my creepiest creep.

All About Me
Ethan G.
Ms. French, 5th Grade

I am a kid with blonde hair who is nice.
I wonder what job I will have.
I hear my brother yell when I shoot him with a nerf gun.
I see my house when I come home.
I want Sprite right now.
I am a kid with blonde hair who is nice.

I pretend to sleep when I am annoyed.
I feel tired when I go to school.
I touch the air when I am outside.
I worry about falling off a cliff.
I cry when people die.
I am a kid with blonde hair who is nice.

I understand I have good grades.
I say get out to my brother.
I dream about being killed.
I hope I get good grades.
I am a kid with blonde hair who is nice.

Chapter 9
Odds and Ends

Sister Anne's Hands
Carlina M.
Ms. Ryan, 3rd Grade

Mrs. Ryan read about <u>Sister Anne's Hands </u>by Mary Beth Lorbiecki. I made a connection to the book that Mrs. Ryan read. It was that I have a favorite teacher, too and it is Mrs. Ryan. She is my favorite teacher in the whole wide world. That is how I made a connection about the book. Mrs. Ryan is kind, sweet, and pretty like Sister Anne in the book. She is also fun to have for a teacher.

Monster Trucks
Jacob E.
Ms. Ryan, 3rd Grade

I like monster trucks because they are big and cool. My brother has a D.S. with a game where you drive a monster truck. It is fun to play monster trucks. When I feel like I'm in it. I play it every day. I like it so much. I want to drive one. Do you? If you do, keep reading because that is just the beginning of it. I want to play the Wii because I have a Nascar game. I can unlock a monster truck on it but I can't play it every day.

Flat Stanley Goes to Hollywood
Simone B.
Ms. Ryan, 3rd Grade

Hi, I'm Flat Stanley. Today is a special day. Guess where I'm going? I'm going to Hollywood with my brother, Arther, and my other flat friends, Flat Jr., and Flat Flatty. Flat Jr. is not very flat but he'll work.

On the first day to Hollywood Flat Stanley flew out the window. A woman screamed so hard he was falling on the ground and was cracking up.

Connections
Korey C.
Ms. Ryan, 3rd Grade

I made a text to self connection with the book The Other Side by Jacqueline Woodson. I liked the book a lot. I thought it was interesting. It can teach people how to be nice and how to make friends like Clover did. Also, the conclusion that I made was that on the book Anne got to do stuff that Clover didn't get to do. In my life, somebody got to do something that my mom wouldn't let me do.

Webkins
Breanna G.
Ms. Ryan, 3rd Grade

I have 22 Webkins and all of them are mine but sometimes I share with my sister and my friends. I try to keep the Webkins away from dogs and cats because if you lay them somewhere a dog and a cat might tear them up. That's way I keep things away from dogs and cats- just in case. The best place to hide them is the closet. I think that sharing is the best way to make friends and to show friendship.

Connections
Ansley W.
Ms. Ryan, 3rd Grade

I heard the story The Other Side, by Lorbiecki and I really liked it. At the beginning, Clover always sees the same girl sitting on the fence. The second day it was raining and she saw her splashing in puddles beside the fence. The third day she was on the fence. One of my connections is that I like to sit the fence like Annie did. The other connection that I have is I have a friend that has the same name. The last connection is that she is black, too. I think what's going to happen is that both of their moms are going to allow them over the fence.

Sports
Sydney W.
Ms. Ryan, 3rd Grade

Hi, I'm Sydney and I play soccer. To play soccer you usually have a special uniform for your team. They can be like your school colors or something like that. You also have to put on special shoes called cleats.

There are exercises in soccer like push- ups, jumping jacks, and stuff like that. But the most important thing is aiming the ball. To aim the ball you need good eye site. I you don't have good eye site, you can't score. If you can't score, then you can't win the game.

Connections
Trinity T.
Ms. Scarbrough, 3rd Grade

When I read the book called <u>Because of Winn Dixie</u> I had made a lot of text-to-self connections. I will be comparing and contrasting me and Opal. This book is about a little girl named Opal. Opal didn't have many friends. She has a mom that ran away.

Opal and I have similar things in common. Opal and I both have moms that like to hear stories. I also have dogs that are scared of storms. Opal and I like to go to church too. Also we both like to go to the library.

Opal and I have a lot of different things about us. I have two parents. Opal has one parent. She lives in a trailer park and I have a house that is in a neighborhood. I have 5 dogs and Opal has 1 dog.

I really loved this book. I like this book because it kind of reminds me of my life. I think this is a good book for kids to read.

The People I Admire
Gavin W.
Ms. Armstrong, 4th Grade

I admire my cousin Brad, my parents, and my grandparents.

I really admire my cousin Brad because he is awesome. We do lots of things together. We bowl, fish, sled, and play sports. Whenever I lose a game, he does not make me feel bad about myself. He is a great cousin.

My parents are two wonderful people. They're nice, they care about me, and they are so loving. We do a lot of fun things as a family. We go to Six Flags, we bowl, and go fishing. They are great people.

I also admire my grandparents. They always take me out to eat when I am hungry. We also watch television and play games together. I love them very much.

So as you can see I truly have some great people to admire in my life.

Dear Grandparents
Amanda C.
Ms. Murdock, 3rd Grade

I wonder if you can come over for Mother's Day. Also I missed you very much. Do you remember the time that it was my birthday and you said that you were doing to get me something? Thank you for that shirt that you bought me. I really like it.

I want you to come over for Mother's Day because I got you something. Also I like those two dresses you got for me. My family was asking if you can call us. So, when are you coming? I hope you have a nice time. I love you very much.

Before you come over I want you to get me a lot of books because I love to read. Buy me lots of books and then I will have plenty of books. I am in third grade now. Last night for dinner I had rice with beef. Grandparents, did you know my dad arranged my room?

For Christmas I got a Wii, Connect Four, boots, a doll, and a jacket.

When I grow up I am going to be a basketball player. For my birthday I got a DS game and clothes. I went to the doctor and got a shot but it didn't hurt.

From, Amanda

Letter to a Substitute
Autum M.
Ms. Armstrong, 4th Grade

Dear Substitute,

This is what you need to know. Our class is very unique so there are some things you need to know.

First, when the students come into the classroom everyone will need to unpack. Sometimes we will be given a worksheet for morning work. When we are finished we would take a restroom break. After that we learn lessons in social studies, language arts, or science.

After we do all of that we would go to specials which may be P.E, computer lab, music, or art. After specials it is lunch time. Then math class. After math we pack up and ago home. And that is how you teach Mrs. Armstrong's class.

Sincerely, Autum M.

The Move
Cason B.
Ms. Murdock, 3rd Grade

Dear Daniel,
 I'm having a lot of fun at this new school. I've made a lot of new friends too. I've learned a lot of new stud. I've learned multiplication and division.
 The playground is different too. It has different swings. Sometimes we play indoor recess because it's either rainy or cold outside.
 My classroom is great. It has mostly everything you need for school.
 If you get a dog tag you get to check out any book in the library. Every month you get a slip so you can check out any book, but we have plenty of books in the classroom. We have Captain Underpants, Magic Tree House, Spiderwick Chronicles, and lots more.
 We have a thing called Math Minute. It's when you do multiplication in one minute. There are twenty-three levels you have to pass. When you're done with multiplication you have to start division.
 Every other Friday we have to go to specials because our teachers have a meeting.
 That's how my school is.
From, Cason

A Continuation of "The Boys Start the War" by Phyllis Reynolds Naylor
Holden H.
Ms. Elmer, 4th Grade

 The boys asked their mom if the girls could spend the night. Their mom said it was fine. Then they played a couple board games and watched TV. Then the boys' mom came into their room. Mom said, "Let the girls sleep in your beds, and you boys make a pallet on the floor."
 They were mad that the girls slept in their beds. They decided to turn all the lights off in the house and jump on all the beds that the girls were sleeping in so the girls would wake up screaming. The boys love playing pranks on the girls, but, when they did, the girls got them back with even better tricks. The

boys wanted to make their trick so evil that the girls wouldn't be able to get them back. Then they came up with an idea. They decided to go over to the girl's house and play a trick on them there instead. They wanted the girls to be so scared that they wouldn't play a prank on them ever again; they would just stay home and watch TV. They wouldn't even say a word to them at school.

A Continuation of "The Boys Start the War" by Phyllis Reynolds Naylor
Mackenzie P.
Ms. Elmer, 4th Grade

Eddie Malloy lay sprawled across her bed thinking of what she was going to do today when suddenly an idea popped into her head. With a laugh she raced downstairs and into the kitchen where her mom and dad were.

Eddie Malloy hopped up and down and said, "Please, please, please! Can we go camping by the river?"

"Well...I guess you can but we have to come with you."

"Ok," said Eddie. Eddie ran into the living room where her two sisters were. Caroline, the youngest had hopes to see her name in lights on Broadway. Beth, the middle-aged one who loved reading long books. Once she got her nose in a book she could not get it out. Eddie told her sisters so excited and how she was going to invite the boys.

Caroline interrupted, "I thought you hate the boys."

"I know, Caroline but we're going to knock them into the river when they're fishing."

"But what if they don't go fishing?" Caroline said.

"They will Caroline. They will," Eddie said.

When they were getting ready to go to the river Eddie called the boys to see if they wanted to go. They said Ok and hung up. Jake and his brothers Josh, Wally, and Peter all gathered around and Jake said, "We're going fishing and with the girls."

Peter said, "I thought you didn't like the girls Jake."

"I know, but we're going to trick the girls. We're going to take their shoes."

"Cool!" said Josh. The boys came out of the house and to the river where the girls were waiting. "Sorry we're late. We had to pack. Did you bring a fishing pole?"

"No," said Wally.

"Ok then. Here you are!"

"Alright," said Jake. "I'm going fishing."

"Ok," said Eddie and her sisters.

While the boys were fishing Eddie whispered, "Perfect!" Eddie and her sisters went over and splash! They all went in except little Peter. When the boys got out and dry the boys went for the shoes. They grabbed them, put them in their bag, and acted normal again.

The next day they said their goodbyes and went home. As soon as the boys were back they called the girls. They said, "We have your shoes."

"Oh no!" Eddie said. "I had forgotten about them. We will get them back. Just wait and see."

My Favorite Novel
Nacirema U.
Ms. French, 5th Grade

The novel I love to read is "The Witches." The main characters in this book are the narrator, a boy whose name is not mentioned, and his grandmother. His grandmother is his guardian because his parents are deceased. She is from Norway and was a professional witchopile. Witchopile means witch catcher. She knows a lot about witches. The other characters are witches. There is a Grand High witch. She and her other witches plan to turn all children into mice! In this book witches don't look like the ones in fairy tales. The witches have no ridiculous pointy hats or broom sticks. They look very ordinary in public, but in private they look very out of the ordinary. Their hats hide their bald heads, their gloves cover their clawed hands, their shoes are wrapped around their toeless feet, and they talk carefully to hide their blue tongues. When the boy and his grandmother find out the witches are up to something, they make a plan to get rid of those horrifying witches once and for all!

Before the boy's father and mother died, they wrote in their will that they wanted the boy to move to England. The grandmother was frightened because all of the most horrifying witches roamed there, but nevertheless they moved there anyway. While living with his grandmother, the boy heard stories about the witches almost every day and he always believed them. His grandmother told him all the things that would show whether or not a lady was a witch, but she warned him that he may not always be able to tell if a lady is really a witch. She also told him witches hated children and would try anything to get rid of them. She told him witches could sniff children out and could sense if children were near, even when the children were squeaky clean. To the witches, children smelled like dog droppings. To make it harder for the witches to smell the boy, his grandmother told him to only bathe once a month. She told him a story about how a witch made a girl go into a painting and she could never get out. The strange thing was, every time the family would look at the picture, the girl would be in a different place and she would age. One day she was no longer in the painting. Some say she died.

One day when the boy was climbing a tree, a lady told him if he came down out of the tree she would give him the snake she was carrying. He thought that he had come across a witch! When he told his grandmother about the lady, she said he definitely met a witch. The grandmother told him if he would have come down, the witch would have tried to do atrocious things to him. That was his first encounter with a witch.

The boy's second encounter with a witch happened while he and his grandmother were on vacation. When they arrived at the hotel, the grandmother surprised the boy with two white mice in a cage. She warned him that he can only play with them if he played someplace no one could see him. As soon as the boy had a hold of the white mice, he thought of being in a mouse circus and traveling the world. The boy decided to train the mice, so he searched for a place where he can hide and train his mice. He found a ballroom and it had RSPCC at the entrance. TSPCC stood for Royal Prevention of Cruelty to Children. The boy thought that if he snuck in there and got caught, the people wouldn't mind because they liked children. When the boy was training his mice, he saw a lot of women come into the room. He was very close to coming out of hiding, then the leader of all the women started to yell. She ordered them to take off their gloves, wigs, and shoes. The boy was horrified when he saw that they were all witches! He was sure glad that he hadn't bathed for a month!

The boy decided to listen in on the witches so he could tell his grandmother the exact location where the Grand Witch lived if they discussed it. When the boy was listening, he heard that they had a secret formula and planned to turn all children into mice. Their plan was to insert the secret formula into candy, and give the candy to the children. The candy would take effect the next day after the children ate it. The parents wouldn't suspect it was the candy. Though the witch did not discuss where she lived, she did tell the witches where to get the formula. She told them the formula was located in room 454.

Those aren't the only things the boy saw and heard at the meeting. The Grand High Witch wanted to show an example of how the candy worked. She gave a piece of Chocolate to Bruno, a greedy, plump, mean child staying at the same hotel as the boy and his grandmother. The Grand High Witch told Bruno if he came to the ballroom she would give him another piece of chocolate. All the witches got excited and put of their disguises and waited for the boy to come. When Bruno finally came, all of the witches were overjoyed, but were warned to behave. The boy was very frightened when he saw Bruno turn into a mouse! All the witches struggled to stomp on Bruno, but he made it into a hole in the wall. Suddenly, one out of the 200 witches stood up and said, "Does anyone smell that? I smell dog droppings!" Suddenly all the witches started looking and smelling around for him. The boy was scared and did not know what to do. Before he was able to think of an idea, a witch screamed, "I found the child in the ballroom! He really stinks!" The witches grabbed the boy and put a large amount of mouse formula in his mouth so the effect on him will happen sooner. The boy soon got smaller and hairier and finally, he turned into a mouse! The boy ran for his life on his scrawny legs!

When the boy finally was in a safe area and all the witches had gone their separate ways. The boy tried to yell for Bruno, but all that came out was a squeak! He tried again because he knew he still had his voice. He finally found Bruno eating a crumb. The boy said to Bruno, "We need to go back to my grandmother's hotel room right now!"

"What about my mother and father?" asked Bruno.

"We'll tell them later but right now let's find our way to my hotel room." When the boy and Bruno were going to his grandmother's hotel room, they had to stay near the wall. It was difficult trying to find their way and avoid getting stomped on by one of the guests. Things had a different view as a mouse. When the boy and Bruno reached their way to the room, they faced another obstacle; they couldn't open the door. Luckily, the grandmother was stepping out and the boy and Bruno had to scream to the grandmother to get her to see them. When the grandmother saw them she screamed also! The grandmother looked very frightened and closed the door quickly so no one could see that the boy and Bruno were in the palm of her hand as mice. The grandmother had already guessed that it was the witches before the boys could even say anything! When the boys explained what happened, they also told her the information about the formula. The grandmother knew that this was maybe their only chance to overcome the witches!

The boy thought that maybe they should give Bruno back to his parent even though he was a mouse. When the grandmother went to Bruno's parents and tried to explain to them that Bruno had been transformed into a mouse, they thought she was insane and shooed her away! So they just decided they would try another time.

The boy reminded the grandmother that the witch said the formula was in hotel room 454. When they went to look at the room, he saw two frogs and followed them. He thought that if he followed them, they would lead him to the formula! That's exactly what the frogs did. As soon as he found the formula, a witch came in and seemed to be looking for something. The boy remembered the Grand High Witch saying to come to her room to get a formula. The boy became sad thinking the witch may find him or take the formula. He became happy when he saw that the witch only came in the hotel room to get the frogs. After the witch left, he got the formula and signaled to his grandmother to pull him back up to their hotel room. When the grandmother saw that the boy got the formula, she went into phase two but first they tried to introduce Bruno to his parents again. When they tried again, Bruno's parents assumed the grandmother was bizarre so the left Bruno's parents home and started phase two of their plan.

They heard that all the witches were going to have dinner with the owner of the hotel at 6:00 pm (even though the Grand High Witch called him an ignorant fool). They set out to the hotel restaurant to see what the witches were ordering. They were frightened al the witches would order all various foods, making phase two of the plan difficult. Luckily all of the witches ordered the same food; soup. Since the boy was now small, he could easily sneak into the soup pot and pour the mouse formula in, and he did. Some of the cooks saw him when he was on the way back to his grandmother, and were trying to kill him. He made it back to his grandmother unharmed. He snuck into her bag, relaxed, and watched the witches sip their soup and turn into mice. After that, the boy and his grandmother traveled the world to get rid of witches once and for all.

"The Witches" is a book everyone should read. It is a book that is enjoyable at any age, but reading this book is the only way children will ever want to meet the witches!

A New Horizon
Danielle Cochran (5ᵗʰ Grade Teacher)
Written on April 4, 1997

Every day I take at least one hour to come sit under the big oak tree behind my house. I sit here and think. Sometimes I think about people, dreams, or events that happened in the past. My mother tells me that I think too much. Maybe she is right, but without anyone to talk to, it is the only thing to do.

Today I am thinking about something that happened yesterday morning. It has really puzzled me. I awoke at six o'clock yesterday morning to go to the oak tree. I had to go early because I planned to be gone all day. I pulled on my favorite t-shirt and a pair of jeans. After brushing my teeth and doing all of the necessary procedures to get ready, I headed for the door. The sun was beginning to peek over the horizon. The color combination of the sunrise was awkwardly different. The light coming from the sun nearly blinded me as I walked outside. I could not see anything because of the heavy blanket of mist that filled the air but, I had walked the path leading to the tree hundreds of times. I knew where to go. I walked slowly, trying to feel my way around. It seemed as if I walked forever!

After about thirty minutes of tripping over rocks and dodging trees, I fell down a little step that I had never noticed before. It took me a few minutes to restore myself, but I was not hurt. When I looked up, I saw the most beautiful place in the world. It had wonderful green trees, fountains of water, and fresh air everywhere. It is very hard to describe the beauty of this place. It was a world of which I could only dream. I went to the edge of a small stream nearby, kneeled down, and splashed some of the crystal clear water on my face to make sure I was not dreaming. After realizing it was not a dream, I stood up. I saw a girl walking toward me. She had long, beautiful hair and a gorgeous dress. She told me her name was Conny and that I was in the Land of Thinkers. She explained that I was here because of my meditative ways. The tree, which I sit by every day, was planted millions of years ago for people like me who need a place to relax and think. Conny said that whenever someone sits by the tree and thinks, the people of this land hear their thoughts and therefore, learn new things. After one thousand thoughts, a person was brought to this temporary "concentration" camp to be praised and rewarded. The person, which is me, was granted one wish and until I could decide what to wish for, I was treated like a queen.

After many helpings of fresh fruit and pure water, I decided what to wish for. I went to Conny and told her that I wished for a best friend; someone to talk to and go places with; someone who liked me for who I am. Conny wasn't very happy with what I wished for. She was afraid that I would forget to think if I had a friend. If I did not think, the thinkers could not learn. I pleaded and tried very hard to convince her to grant my wish. When she had had enough of my begging, she ordered me to leave. She showed me how to get back home. I went slowly.

Once on Earth's soil again, I turned around and watched the sun, which was now normal, rise into the bright blue sky. As I walked to my house, I was very sad that my wish was not granted, and I cried myself to sleep once I was in my bed. I awoke at six o'clock again this morning and came out here to watch the sun slowly rising over the horizon. I suppose I will never know whether I dreamed what happened yesterday, or not. It may not sound realistic, but as I am looking at the horizon right now, I see a girl about my age walking my way. A friend?

Letter of Appreciation
Ms. Partains 4th Grade Class

Dear American Hero,

We would like to take this opportunity to thank you for the things you have sacrificed to defend our country. Giving up time with family, friends, and loved ones is a great price to pay. You are in our thoughts during the holiday season. We support you and thank you for all that you do.

Sincerely,
Ms. Partain's
4th Grade Class

Computers
Taylor A.
Ms. French, 5th Grade

Do you like to have fun on the computer? I absolutely love playing on the computer. One of the things I like to do on the computer is emailing my friends. Another thing I adore is playing games. Next, you can use it for school resources. Last but not least, is if there is an emergency yo can tell someone faster. Wow! Computers have changed the world.

Emailing is fun and fast. It is a faster way to talk to your friends. It is very easy to email. All you have to do is type in a message. Then you type in who you want. Finally press the send button on your keyboard. It happens quick as a wink.

Games, board games, DS games, and GameBoys are fun, but I love computer games. Some games come in disks. Some games are already on the computer. Some you have to download. MySpace, FaceBook, Club Penguin, WebKins, etc. are all games that already come on the computer. There is a whole world of fun available to you at a touch of a button.

School is another thing you can use the computer for. If you don't know the meaning of a word you can look it up. When my parents were younger, they had to go to a library to do any research. All the research I need is just a click away. Our school also has a lot of interesting programs such as PebbleGo, TumbleBooks, World Book Online. It is unbelievable how much information is available to me.

Computers, in my opinion are the best invention ever. They have changed the world. I wonder if computers can get any better.

Breakfast
Isabella W.
Ms. French, 5th Grade

What is your favorite meal of the day? Eating breakfast every day is a habit everyone needs to get into for many reasons. First, breakfast is really healthy for you. Second, it's the most important meal of the day. Third, it keeps us full until lunch. So let's start the stove!

First, breakfast is very good for you. Children and even adults are always complaining that their stomachs hurt, but right when they eat something they feel fine. When you think of healthy, you probably think of vegetables, although eggs, toast, and fruit are just as beneficial. Lots of different foods have calcium, vitamins, and good calories that help us grow and stay well. Breakfast is a perfect opportunity to be creative and healthy.

Second, this meal is the most important. Scientists are always saying that this meal is super-necessary because it gives your body fuel for the whole day. Eating breakfast in the morning always helps you concentrate.

Third, you'll be full until lunch. Your stomach will be satisfied and not upset or hurting. Headaches normally happen when you haven't eaten anything. You don't have to worry about being hungry. You'll be full and you can learn, grow, and succeed.

Breakfast should be an essential part of your day. Whether it is cereal, fruit, eggs, or pancakes it is the perfect tool to start your day off on the right foot.

Index of Authors

Edmund H. 32
Elizabeth M. 82
Ellington L. 6
Elliott L. 3
Elyssa J. 64
Emily D. 157
Emily F. 157
Emma B. 158
Emma P. 59
Emma W. 7
Emmet L. 11
Erin B. 61
Esther R. 1
Esther R. 2 artwork
Ethan C. 2
Ethan G. 13
Ethan G. 141
Ethan G. 166
Ethan H. 156
Ethan R. 156
Evan G. 67
Eymbrie P. 6
Gabriella C. 85
Gage J. 30
Garret G. 58
Gary S. 33
Gavin S. 8
Gavin W. 170
Georgia R. 1
Grace G. 88
Grace G. 148
Grace K. 12

Gracen B. 97
Graham G. 8
Griffin L. 125
Griffin L. 137
Hailey H. 12
Halee M. 5
Haley A. 109
Haley C. 5
Hannah I. 33
Hannah S. 6
Hayli B. 78
Holden H. 172
Hope B. 101
Hunter B. 5
Hunter C. 69
Hunter G. 8
Hunter S. 3
Ian C. 36
Ireland B. 155
Isabella W. 145
Isabella W. 181
Izsak S. 2
Jack N. 126
Jack N. 140
Jackson H. 4
Jackson L. 79
Jacob E. 167
Jacob K. 157
Jacob M. 52
Jacob M. 158
Jada C. 50
Jake H. 1

LaVergne, TN USA
19 April 2010
179738LV00003B/7/P